A FLAME
IN THE WIND

Other books by Karen Cogan:

The Secret of Castlegate Manor

A FLAME
IN THE WIND

•

Karen Cogan

AVALON BOOKS
NEW YORK

PRINTED IN THE UNITED STATES OF AMERICA
ON ACID-FREE PAPER
BY HADDON CRAFTSMEN, BLOOMSBURG, PENNSYLVANIA

I would like to dedicate this book in memory of my mother, Kathryn, and to my father, Hugh, sister, Carolyn and brother, Richard, and their families for all their kind encouragement.

Chapter one

Rebecca stretched her stiff muscles as the coach rolled to a stop to take on a new passenger. Two days of jolting along rutted bush trails had bruised her bones and left her longing for a bath and fresh clothes. However, the shacks in the tiny towns where they had stopped possessed no facilities for a bath.

Now, as the cool of morning ebbed, a sultry stuffiness filled the inside of the coach and made her thin cotton dress cling to her damp body.

Rebecca brushed aside her discomfort, consoling herself with the progress she had made. The thick forests surrounding Sydney had faded far into the eastern horizon. The rough trail over the Blue Mountains lay behind them and the grasslands stretched ahead. The trip would be over soon, and the result would be worth the discomfort. The thick forest would no longer engulf her, nor the dark house where she had spent the last eight years.

She smiled at the young woman who entered the coach, glad for female company. She had shared the first leg of the trip with a grizzled prospector who had repeated a tale of wealth quickly gained and as quickly lost while mining

Summerhill Creek. He had finally been overtaken by his gin and fallen asleep.

Rebecca let the young woman settle in her seat before introducing herself and saying, "I'll be stopping at Bathurst. How about you?"

The newcomer regarded her with wary curiosity. Her dark eyes held cat-like caution. Her broad face, accentuated by auburn waves of hair spilling out from her bonnet, was attractive, if not pretty.

"I'm Anna Simpson," the girl replied. "I'm headed for a job in Bathurst." She took in Rebecca's faded dress, less patched than her own. "What will you be doing there?"

"I'm meeting my father. He has a ranch outside of town. It's been years since I've seen him." Rebecca's voice trembled as she anticipated the reunion.

Anna nodded. "I expect your father will be relieved to see you this afternoon. He must be worried to have a daughter like you traveling through bushranger territory. I've been worried myself for fear of being held up. Not that I have anything."

Anna sounded bitter. Rebecca wondered why, and pitied her.

She told Anna, "I've waited years to come home. I'd risk even bushrangers."

"It must be nice to have a home." Anna pointed to the cask of gin beside the snoring passenger. "Gin robbed me of any home I could have had."

Rebecca studied her a moment before she softly said, "I'm so sorry. Is anyone meeting you in town?"

Anna shook her head. Any hint of openness melted from her face. "I'll get a job. I don't need anyone to take care of me."

Rebecca nodded, recognizing Anna's desire to take care of herself. Rebecca had nearly suffocated under her aunt's tyrannical guardianship. She, too, welcomed the opportunity for freedom.

After a moment, Anna's expression softened. "I didn't mean to be short with you, but please, I don't want to talk about myself. Tell me about your father."

Rebecca thought Anna could not be a day older than herself. Yet, she spoke to her as she might to a child. For the sake of companionship, Rebecca decided to ignore the offense and share the pleasant memories of her childhood.

"I remember how Father walked home each day from tending sheep. I'd run to him and he'd dust his hat against his leg before he swept me into his arms. His blue eyes would sparkle and he would ask, 'What's my darlin' done for mischief?' "

Rebecca chuckled at the memory. "I'd laugh and deny any wrongdoing. But every day I'd usually done something to cause my mother grief. The dingo pup I lured home tore the linen from the clothesline that stretched from the house to a bottle tree. The lizards and other creatures I brought into the house were a constant irritation to Mother."

She sighed. "Finally, it was all too much. Mother insisted on passage back to Sydney for a visit to my aunt, Abigail."

Anna frowned. "That must have been hard for you."

Rebecca shook her head. "At first I was excited at the chance to visit the city. However, when the visit became an extended stay, the truth sunk in. After a few months, Father made the trip once by wagon to beg Mother to return."

Rebecca choked back the resentment that welled in her chest. "He might as have saved the trouble. My aunt turned him away at the door."

She took a deep breath and continued. "It upset me terribly, but Mother didn't care. She loved the social life of Sydney and she let too much gin ruin her looks and her health."

Anna nodded vigorously. Her dark hair bounced on her shoulders. "That's just like my folks, 'cept it was both of them. Never cared a lick for me, just for the gin."

"It's a terrible thing," Rebecca agreed. "My aunt humored Mother like she was a child. She blamed my father for Mother's ruin, though it was really her own weakness. And my aunt ruled me with an iron hand and a switch."

Rebecca shivered at the memory. Her aunt's strictness had bordered on cruelty. She kept Rebecca confined to the house and filled her time with cleaning, studying, and taking in other people's laundry. She kept all the money Rebecca earned, adding it to the ample store of coins she had inherited and now hoarded. Once a week she allowed Rebecca to attend church.

Rebecca would have found Abigail's tyranny impossible to endure if not for her weekly outings. Each week, she renewed her hope that her life would not be spent in misery under her aunt's thumb. She spent the next four years shielding that hope like a flame caught by the wind.

Abigail's demands kept Rebecca constantly busy. When her mother fell ill from a respiratory disease, Rebecca became her nurse. When she died, Rebecca wrote her father. He could not hope to arrive in time for the funeral and would not be welcomed by her aunt if he came afterwards. Still, Rebecca thought he deserved to know.

His return letter reached her a month later. Her hope to regain happiness lay in the neatly scripted invitation to return home along with money for passage. She had clutched the letter in her hands when she faced her aunt Abigail with her decision.

Bitterness showed in the old woman's eyes. "You'll come to a bad end in that Godforsaken land."

Rebecca faced her squarely. "You needn't worry for me. Father will see to me."

Abigail's laugh was sarcastic and thin. "As he saw to your mother? It was her ruin to marry him and leave Sydney. It will be your ruin, too." She followed with a barrage of warnings about prodigal sons and foolish servants.

Rebecca caught her lip between her teeth and waited,

willing herself to have patience until her aunt grew tired of the tirade. At last Abigail fell silent and regarded Rebecca with sharp eyes that reminded Rebecca of an angry parrot's.

Rebecca licked her lips and spoke softly. "I know you don't agree with my decision to return to the sheep station. However, I feel it is where I am meant to go. And I will go."

Her boldness with the woman who had ruled her life brought a sweet rush of freedom. Nothing her aunt could say or do would stand in her way. Rebecca was twenty years old and had passage money in hand.

When she left the next day, she received no farewell or good wishes from Abigail. She had not expected any. Rebecca gave a backward glance to the decaying old house that had been her prison as she set her sights to the future.

Anna leaned forward, drawing Rebecca's thoughts back to the present. "From first looking at you, I thought you'd lived a soft life. Guess I was wrong."

Rebecca smiled. "There was always plenty of work." She stretched her hands to reveal her reddened knuckles as proof she had not been idle. Her hands were large and strong for a woman, with long, tapered fingers.

"So your father sent for you?" Anna asked.

Rebecca nodded as she drew her father's letter from her pocket. It was dated August 4, 1856, four weeks before she had begun her trip. She had read it so many times that it was creased and faded. Yet prickles of expectancy rose on the back of her neck as she smoothed the wrinkled paper.

"I could never have afforded the passage. Father spent the last eight years saving from the wool sales to give me a chance to come back. He sent the money along with this letter."

She opened the letter and scanned the lines that told how he had missed her and the pain he had felt upon hearing that her mother had died. He had never given up hope that they might be a family again, though he knew in his heart that his wife had never been meant for the lonely bush.

Rebecca had written immediately, telling him which stage she had booked for passage. Now, nearing the end of the three-day trip, she could hardly believe she was nearly home. She turned her attention to the tawny hills and quartz outcroppings that lay on the horizon. The town of Bathurst loomed ahead.

Rebecca's heartbeat quickened. She longed to bury her fingers in soft wool as she helped her father shear. She longed to ride the banks of the Macquarie River, looking for straggler sheep sneaking a last drink. But most of all, she longed to see her father. Had he changed much in the years since she'd seen him?

It didn't matter. She couldn't wait to see the sparkle in his blue eyes. She couldn't wait to feel the comfort of his hug. When she saw him, she would know she was truly home.

The coach ground to a stop, interrupting her thoughts. The horses stamped, eager to be released from their harness. The driver opened the coach door, and Anna rose from her seat.

"Where will you go?" Rebecca asked.

Anna bit her lip, and then nodded toward the saloon. "Don't worry about me. I've worked saloons before."

Rebecca drew a surprised breath. Still, she hated to let their budding friendship die. "I'll write to you. Will you write back?"

"Dalton, right?"

"Yes."

"I'll try, though my spelling's not too good."

Before Rebecca could reply, Anna said, "Have a good reunion with your father."

Rebecca watched her disappear down the wobbly steps that had been set beside the stage. She followed and watched as Anna collected her bags and hurried toward the saloon.

Rebecca grasped her cloth satchel. Her lips parted in a tentative smile as she glanced along the dusty street. Several men lounged outside the saloon, admiring Anna as she passed through the swinging doors. Rebecca did not see her father.

She brushed back her flaxen hair and put her hand to her forehead to block the afternoon sun as she scanned the trail that led the fifteen miles to her ranch. Perhaps her father had not received her letter telling of her arrival.

She sighed. It was too late to attempt a walk. She would have to go into the livery and make other arrangements.

Her eyes locked onto those of a stranger, a well-built young man with dark eyes. He stood rigid as a post near a hitching rail. Her smile faded as he continued his solemn scrutiny of her. She deliberately turned from the intensity of his stare, hoping to see her father appear down the road. He was nowhere in sight.

Rebecca didn't know how painfully the young man's heart thumped in his chest at the anxiety growing on her delicate face. Though they'd never met, Cole knew with certainty that she was Rebecca Dalton. He knew he should end her confusion.

Cole McBride was a man strengthened from childhood by hard work and hardship. Yet he could not will a single muscle to move. Her hopeful face rendered him helpless. As she peered down the road, he realized this meeting was going to be even harder than he'd expected.

Cole forced himself to leave the hitching post. He couldn't let her linger in confusion any longer. He set his jaw in determination and took a step forward.

"Miss Dalton?"

Rebecca whirled and fixed him with sky-blue eyes. Cole felt himself flinch. He licked his dry lips. "I'm Cole McBride. I've been sent to fetch you."

Her face showed momentary relief. "My father couldn't come?" Her voice had the clarity of a songbird and the lilt of a girl educated in the city.

Cole shook his head. A wave of sorrow surged through his chest. He would have done anything to have the power to reverse the past.

He picked up her bags from the dusty ground and headed toward the waiting wagon. Rebecca scurried beside him. "You haven't told me why you're here." Her voice held insistence.

Cole's hands shook as he set the bags in the back of the wagon. "Do you remember G.W.?"

Rebecca nodded. "Yes. He owns the large sheep station next to my father's."

"He asked me to come for you." Cole wished G.W. had come instead. But he knew his employer had not wished to give Rebecca the news. He took a deep breath and plunged ahead. "Your father had an accident. It only happened four days ago. There was no time to get a letter to you before you left."

Rebecca's lips parted with shock, and Cole was again struck by her delicate beauty. She clutched the wagon seat with both hands as she allowed him to help her aboard.

"How bad is he?" Her clear eyes clouded with alarm; the question came as barely more than a whisper.

Cole swung beside her. He could not face her with the terrible answer. He picked up the reins, but made no move to urge the horses forward.

"The hub broke on his wagon when he was coming back from G.W.'s place. He plunged into the ravine. He was killed when his head hit the rocks. I'm sorry, Miss."

He glanced to the side and winced at the horror written on Rebecca's face. Her expression quickly changed to disbelief.

"How could this happen?"

"I don't know. The wagon was solid when he left. I'd swear to that." His voice held deep conviction.

Cole clicked to the team and aimed the horses toward the large sheep station. Rebecca could stay there until she made arrangements to go back to Sydney. He was sure G.W. would see to her funds if she were short of passage money.

Rebecca buried her face in her hands. Her shoulders shook with grief. Cole cursed himself for holding back part of the story, yet there was no way he would yield the admission that would cause her to hate him.

After a time, Rebecca's sobs trailed into numbed silence. She studied the scenery, hoping to reach the ranch and learn that the news had been a horrible mistake. Yet even as she nurtured the hope she knew it couldn't be true.

What would she do, now that she was alone? She could not bear either returning to Sydney or selling the ranch that had meant so much to her father.

The ranch would fall to her. The sudden responsibility felt like a crushing weight. It had been years since she'd been there. Then, she'd been a child, unconcerned with the daily operations. She hoped old Ned was still there. She could count on the aged Scotsman to help her keep things running.

Her thoughts were in confusion as they drove through the gate that led to the ranch house. An aborigine squatted in the dust. He watched them pass, his placid face observing the new arrival with quiet interest.

Rebecca watched the sprawling house loom in front of them. G.W. Sanders had settled with his father a dozen years ago to run a large sheep ranch with convict labor supplied by the government. The elder Sanders had died before Rebecca left for Sydney, leaving the growing ranch to his son. Rebecca had been there several times as a young girl. She remembered G.W. as a stout young man with sandy hair and a round, ruddy face.

G.W. appeared on the porch before Cole could help her from the wagon. His hair had thinned over the years and his face was creased with wrinkles from the unrelenting sun.

Rebecca accepted his outstretched hand. His eyes were warm with sympathy. "I'm sorry, Rebecca. I'd hoped to have a pleasant visit with you when you'd settled with your father at Kangaroo Flats."

Rebecca's eyes filled with tears at her father's name for their ranch. "I can't believe what I was told. Is it true that he's gone?"

G.W. nodded. "The aborigine we call Wally found him near the wagon." He gestured toward the native at the gate who squatted with a woman and young child. Smoke drifted from their small cooking fire.

"I want to see where my father is buried." Rebecca's voice broke as she brushed away the tears that rolled down her cheeks.

A picture of him dusting off his hat came to her mind. She saw herself, a little girl again, running toward him. Suddenly the picture disappeared, leaving her standing alone.

"Certainly. We buried him in the shade of a eucalyptus at the bottom of the knoll. It will be dark soon. It would be best to show you tomorrow."

Rebecca nodded and fought to regain her composure.

G.W. took her bags from Cole and escorted her into the house. His sandy brows furrowed with concern. "You've had quite a shock. You should stay here tonight."

Rebecca stood uncertainly. She really had little choice, and she was thirsty and unbearably tired. She forced a smile. "I would appreciate your hospitality."

G.W.'s broad face lit with a gentle grin. "I'll cart your bags to the back room and be straight back. Do have a sit."

Rebecca sank onto the settee carved from the trunk of a bottle tree. The warmth had vanished from the setting sun, and a sallow haze captured the dust dancing in the air. Uncurtained windows stared down at Rebecca like pitiless eyes. A hand-hewn coffee table sat before her. The rich grain of the wood, beautiful when bathed in light, was hidden in shadow.

When G.W. returned, the old bushman who had long served as his cook set roasted mutton on the table. Rebecca joined G.W. Though she had little appetite for food, she gratefully accepted a cup of strong coffee.

Throughout supper G.W. kept up a steady stream of conversation about his ranch. It was plain that pride in his legacy had spurred him to impressive improvements. Rebecca listened quietly, grateful for the discourse that spared her the need to talk.

As the cook cleared the dishes, G.W. fixed her with an uncertain look. "I guess you'd like to turn in now."

Rebecca nodded. "I would."

Her grief had threatened to spill forward all through supper, and she welcomed the chance to be alone. In the privacy of a bedroom, she could unleash the pain she'd struggled to hold in check.

G.W. led her down a short hall to a room furnished with a bed and a large chest. Rebecca stepped into the room. A fireplace sat in one corner. She would have no need of it on this early spring night. She turned her back to G.W. to hide the tears that spilled down her face.

G.W. hesitated in the doorway. "It's a big house for a man alone. I've always thought someday I'd marry and have a passel of kids. I might even have to add on a few rooms." His voice was wistful, but Rebecca was too torn by grief to carefully consider his words.

"I'm in the next room if you should need anything." He closed the door softly and left her alone.

Not bothering to undress, Rebecca fell across the bed and dropped her head onto her arms. She let the grief and shock wash over her, feeling as abandoned as a little child.

She sobbed until anger edged into her grief. Unreasonable anger at her father and the uncertainties of life gripped her. She had waited eight years to come back, only to be cheated from the homecoming she had acted out a thousand times in her imagination as she scrubbed floors or hung out wash.

She pounded the bed in helpless frustration. She longed to scream like a wounded animal and shatter the night silence. Yet she dared not vent her anger until she reached the confines of the little thatched-roof cabin to which she planned to return.

Any commotion she made would surely send G.W. running. It gave her an odd feeling to know he was so close. He was a familiar fixture from her childhood, yet eight years had changed her from a child to a woman. She sensed that G.W. had noticed.

Exhaustion turned her mind into a jumble of disjointed thoughts. She was alone in the world. Her father's absence would complicate her life in the outback. She had already been forced to accept the hospitality of a man who was little more than a stranger to her now.

She closed her eyes, seeking solace in sleep. She longed to wake in the morning and discover that the recent events were all a dream. She would get back on the coach and continue her journey. This time, when she arrived, her father would be waiting.

But that wasn't possible. She remembered all too well the man who had met her with the terrible news. She could still see his eyes, dark eyes that had seemed to reflect her pain.

On the long journey to the ranch, she had sat in numb silence, watching his strong hands guide the team. She could still see those fingers, long and tanned from hours in the sun.

Though she hadn't known him, she'd felt comforted by

his presence. She wondered if she might have enjoyed the trip under different circumstances.

Rebecca searched her mind for his name. *Cole*, she remembered. His face floated in her mind, a handsome face, slender with a strong jaw. Wavy chestnut hair showed from under his broad-brimmed hat. A tiny, jagged scar crept from the edge of his right eye.

Rebecca's grief was tinged by a curiosity to know more about him. Where had he gotten the scar? He didn't seem the type to engage in barroom brawls.

She cradled her curiosity, holding it close like a tiny flame against the whirlwinds that had ripped through her life. She drifted from consciousness with a wish to see Cole again.

Chapter two

Cole lay on his back, staring at the bunkhouse ceiling. He cringed at the yapping of dingoes chasing a hapless creature in the bush. He wondered if Rebecca heard them too.

The outback was no place for the unwary. Old-timers said you never knew the sort of danger you'd meet until it was too late. It was certainly no place for a woman alone.

He expected she would make arrangements to head back to Sydney. G.W. would surely be interested in her father's ranch if she decided to sell.

She could manage nicely in Sydney with the money. And a woman with her looks would have no trouble finding a husband. He was surprised she had not married already.

His mind drifted to her creamy skin and hair the color of white birch that fell straight and smooth, framing her delicate face.

Cole sighed. However she chose to manage her affairs, he would be glad to see her go. Every time he looked at her, he was reminded of his part in causing her pain. He could never look into those eyes, bluer than a cloudless sky, without feeling a double portion of the guilt that tortured him day and night.

Rebecca looked a great deal like her father. Cole had liked Roger Dalton, a good man, honest and hardworking, with a good natured face and friendly blue eyes. Cole wondered if Rebecca were as congenial and concerned for others as Roger had been. It had been impossible to learn much about her in their sorrowful meeting that afternoon.

Cole grimaced in the darkness. If life had been fair, Roger would not have died.

He turned over with an exasperated sigh and tried to shut out the snores of the six ranch hands who shared the bunkhouse. Speculation about Rebecca was pointless. If luck were on his side, she'd be on her way soon and he wouldn't see her again.

He slept fitfully, finally opening his eyes to the voices and rustlings of the other men, who were dressing for breakfast at the ranch house. He sat up and rubbed his eyes, feeling tired from his restless night. Nonetheless, a day's work awaited him. Sheep had to be driven to pasture and the shearing pens needed repair.

Cole glanced into the sky as he stepped from the bunkhouse. A handful of fluffy clouds dotted the distant horizon. Parrots squawked overhead, chasing from tree to tree, while a mob of red kangaroos grazed just beyond the gate.

In the kitchen, Cole poured himself a cup of coffee. G.W. came in as the cook pulled a second pan of biscuits from the oven. The rancher nodded to Cole. "I want an extra gun along when I take Miss Dalton to see her father's grave. Give the men their assignments, then saddle up and come with me."

Cole nearly choked on his coffee. He set the cup down unsteadily, sloshing liquid on top of the plank table as he cast about for a reason not to go.

"I could send one of the men with you. Then I could stay here to see to things," he offered.

G.W. shook his head. "You got the sharpest eyes, near

as good as the aborigines. The men can work without you for awhile."

Cole nodded. Further argument would only serve to rouse G.W.'s curiosity, as well as his irritation. It would be best to grit his teeth and go along. Once Rebecca paid her respects at the gravesite, she could be on her way.

Rebecca had no such plans as she dressed in her riding skirt and long-sleeved blouse to protect her fair skin from the merciless sun. A glance in the mirror told her she wasn't looking her best. Dark rings shadowed her eyes, and her lids were swollen from crying.

She sighed, feeling tired although the day had barely begun. She wished G.W. would let her go alone to mourn at her father's grave. Yet she knew, after all his warnings of danger, he would never agree. And it would be ungracious of her to insist, even though it would force her to contain the feelings she wanted to vent. She longed to rage against the unfairness of the years that had been stolen. But G.W.'s presence would not allow for such display. She would have to return to the site another time without him.

Rebecca splashed cool water on her face and then pulled her hair back with a ribbon. As usual, several fine strands escaped along the sides. She turned from the mirror with a shrug.

"It's not like I'm trying to catch a man's eye," she murmured. Even as she said it, she knew it was not entirely true. She would enjoy a look of approval from Cole. She bit her lip, chastising herself for such an inappropriate thought. He surely wasn't thinking about her.

Cole saddled the horses and waited for Rebecca and G.W. to finish their breakfasts in the dining room. He wasn't prepared for his reaction when Rebecca stepped onto the porch.

He drew a quick breath. He had spent the night convincing himself she was not as beautiful as he remembered. Yet as her blonde hair shimmered in the sunlight and her gaze lingered on his face, Cole knew he had never laid eyes a more enchanting sight.

They mounted the horses and were soon riding toward Roger's ranch. They kept to an easy lope. The waves of grass bent under the horses' hooves, leaving evidence of their passage.

As they entered Roger's pastures, a flock of emu boldly watched them, beaks full of grass meant for sheep. Cole glared at the ungainly creatures and determined to take Wally on another hunt to clear out some of the dim-witted birds. Wally's people could use the meat and the sheep could use the grass.

As the sun rose higher, they slowed the horses to a more leisurely pace. Near the large eucalyptus, G.W. and Cole reined their horses. A small white cross marked a grave beneath the lonely tree.

Rebecca bit her bottom lip as she dismounted. She stared at the marker that bore the name ROGER DALTON. This was pure and unmistakable proof. Her father really was gone.

She walked slowly toward the grave. Tears clouded her eyes, mercifully blurring the name on the cross. She wiped the tears with the back of her hand.

G.W. pointed at the small thatched cottage across the grassy pasture. "I didn't want him to be too far from the house."

She nodded. Tears slipped down her cheeks. "He'd like it here. I couldn't have picked a better spot."

G.W. cleared his throat and stared at his stubby, powerful hands. He seemed uncomfortably unsure of how to comfort her. "We didn't have a minister, so Ned said a few words over the grave."

She swallowed hard. "I'm glad he had a proper burial."

G.W. rubbed his chin. "He was a good man. He had to be to transform an old convict like Ned."

"Ned was always a great help to my father." She stared at the shack attached to the house. There was no point in looking for the old hired hand there now. He would be out with the sheep.

G.W. wiped his damp brow. "Ned promised he'd stay on and run the place as long as you need him."

"He's been a loyal friend. I would never want him to live anywhere else. This is his home."

Cole's eyes darkened with self-reproach. He listened in silence, his heart heavy as stone. So much pain, so many broken dreams. And it was his fault. He gripped his rifle tightly and tried not to listen.

Rebecca knelt and rubbed her hand across the rough wood of the birch cross. "I wish I'd come a few days earlier. I could have spent some time with him before the accident."

"If you don't mind me asking, do you plan to go straight back to Sydney?" G.W. asked.

Rebecca turned with a frown. "I don't plan to ever go back to Sydney." She brushed a stray lock of hair from her cheek. "All I've ever wanted was to come back here. I never cared for life in Sydney."

G.W. took a deep breath. His ruddy face flushed a deeper red. "I'm glad to hear you say that. I've been hoping you'd want to stay. Your father and I had a good many chats about you over the years."

"Oh . . ." Rebecca's eyes widened in interest.

"Yes. It was his hope that you'd want to come back. He remembered how you loved it."

"I did. I still do."

G.W. drew his sandy eyebrows into a frown. "But it's no place for a woman alone. Your father would be the first to agree."

She blinked back a barrage of angry tears. "I don't seem to have a choice."

"But you do. It was your father's hope that you'd marry

a local rancher. We were good friends and he'd hoped that . . . well . . ." G.W. broke off with a self-consciousness blush.

Cole understood G.W.'s intentions now. He wanted to marry Rebecca and have her stay on the big ranch. Cole could certainly understand the older man's attraction to her. He'd felt it himself.

He felt his hands grow clammy. In spite of the disappointment it would cause G.W., Cole hoped she'd turn him down. He couldn't keep working for G.W. if Rebecca came to live on the ranch. It would be too painful.

Rebecca stared at G.W. for a moment, her blue eyes wide as she took in his meaning. Then she slowly shook her head. "You've been a wonderful friend. But I hardly know you. Maybe, in time, we can be more than friends, but now . . ." She spread her hands in a gesture of vulnerability.

G.W. nodded solemnly. "This has all come so sudden, you haven't had time to think. You can stay on at my place. We'll get to know each other. Then maybe you'll decide to stay and get married."

"Your place?" Rebecca repeated. "I'm going home as soon as I get my things."

"Home? But you said you didn't want to return to Sydney," G.W. protested.

Cole's heart beat with an odd combination of regret and relief. There it was. She'd already changed her mind. He knew G.W. was lonely; all men were lonely out here. But G.W. would get over her and life would go back to normal.

"I'm not going to Sydney." Rebecca cocked her head, studying G.W. as though he were slow-witted. "I'm living here at Kangaroo Flats."

G.W. released his breath so rapidly that he looked like a balloon that had suddenly popped. "Alone? You can't mean it."

"I won't be alone. Ned still lives here." Defiance shone in her eyes.

G.W. shook his head. "Ned's getting old. What if there's trouble from the passel of bushmen who come and go for seasonal work?"

Rebecca faced him firmly. "I can manage the workers."

G.W. turned to Cole. "Tell her it's not right."

Cole studied her hard. "It's a crazy idea. You'd be asking for trouble."

Rebecca lifted her chin. Her eyes glinted with determination. If these men thought anything could put aside her years of longing to live at Kangaroo Flats, they were sadly mistaken. "I lived here until I was twelve years old. I can take care of myself."

Cole could almost feel the heat that sparked between them from the conflict. He planted his feet apart, facing her squarely. Two desires competed in his heart. While he longed to protect her from every harm she would face, his common sense told him to pick her up and forcibly deposit her in a coach bound to Sydney.

He surveyed her firm lips, pressed resolutely together. Rebecca's hands rested on her slender waist, her eyes daring him to challenge her decision.

"You're not twelve years old anymore." His voice was cool, his eyes deliberately scanning her slender form. The resulting flush in her cheeks told him she had not missed his point.

He opened his mouth to tell her she had to forget her dreams and accept reality. He stopped cold when he saw a figure slink from behind a bush less than fifty yards away. The man was nearly hidden by the shadow of the ravine where Roger's wagon had gone down. The brief glint of a gun barrel gave Cole no time to shout a warning.

The report of the rifle rent the silence before a bullet slammed G.W. to the ground. Cole reacted instantly, raising his rifle and firing at the shooter, who swung quickly onto a horse and raced up the far side of the ravine.

Cole's shot missed. Instinctively, he spun for his horse,

ready for pursuit. Then he realized G.W. had gone down. If his boss was badly injured, Cole could not afford to lose precious time chasing a man who had a head start.

He knelt beside G.W. as Rebecca pulled away his torn shirt. Blood welled at the rancher's shoulder. His ruddy countenance had paled to a chalky hue, and his eyes were clouded with pain.

Cole felt relief when he saw the wound. It would not be fatal if they could stop the bleeding. He helped Rebecca fold the bottom of G.W's shirt into a flat bandage to press onto the wound.

"We need to get the bullet out. Can you ride?" Cole asked.

G.W. nodded. "I can make it. Did you get a look at who shot me?"

"No." Cole's voice held self-reproach. If he'd paid attention to his job instead of arguing with Rebecca, G.W. might not have been hit.

Supporting him on either side, Rebecca and Cole helped G.W. to his feet and onto his horse. "Keep an eye on him and I'll ride behind as lookout," Cole said.

Rebecca nodded, stunned by the attack. She understood danger. The outback had always held danger. As a child, she'd occasionally heard tales of robbery and murder, usually motivated by money or gin.

The motive for this attack seemed to be murder. But why? Who would want to kill G.W.? she asked herself as their horses plodded along.

She watched G.W. carefully, looking for any sign that he might pass out and slip from his horse. He held his left hand firmly over the wound. Each time she caught his eye, he nodded as though to assure her he would manage. He was tough. She knew that. He had to be tough to survive out here.

Rebecca licked her dry lips. The dust she breathed gave her tongue the gritty texture of sandpaper. She wiped impatiently at the trail of perspiration that trickled down her neck.

It seemed to take forever to reach the arching wooden gate of the ranch. The late morning sun cast a long shadow across their path. The prickle of fear Rebecca carried began to fade. They were nearly back and there had been no further attacks from the gunman.

The ranch looked deserted. The bushmen were out tending the sheep and the cook was inside, busy with lunch preparation. The only sign of human life was Wally, who squatted beside the porch. The aborigine frowned at the blood that seeped through G.W.'s fingers.

Cole jumped from his horse and hurried across the porch. "Davies," he shouted to the cook. "Come out and give us a hand with the boss."

The brawny man emerged with surprising speed. Rebecca held the door while they helped G.W. from his horse. As they half-carried him to the door, Cole called to Wally, "Pick up the tracks in the ravine near Dalton's grave. Find out where they go."

Wally set off at a jog. Rebecca knew natives were expert trackers. If anyone could locate the cowardly gunman, it would be Wally.

They helped G.W. to his bedroom and laid him across the bed. Davies brought clean rags and boiled water while Cole and Rebecca helped G.W. out of his shirt.

Rebecca sponged the wound, grimacing at the sight. The bullet had lodged under G.W.'s skin. She stepped aside to let Cole examine the wound.

"It's not as deep as I feared. But it will have to come out," he said.

G.W. nodded. "Just get me something to bite on."

Cole handed him a wad of cloth, then cleaned a knife and set to work.

Rebecca assisted, cleansing the wound so Cole could see

the path to the bullet. G.W. endured the operation stoically, with only a grunt when Cole dislodged the bullet.

Cole held it for him to see. "That part's over. We'll have to keep the wound clean so you don't get an infection."

Rebecca helped to apply clean bandages and fastened them tightly to G.W.'s chest. When they finished, G.W. struggled to sit up.

Cole eased him gently down. "Better lie flat so you don't bleed too much."

Davies disposed of the shirt and stained rags. He brought a clean basin of water and Cole washed his hands. As the water turned pink, he realized how close he'd come to losing the man who'd helped him when he'd desperately needed a friend.

Men began to drift into the kitchen for lunch. Davies left to finish preparing the food and to explain to the crew what had happened.

Rebecca poured G.W. a cup of water and held it for him to drink.

"Thanks," he said. "You've had a pretty rotten homecoming."

She smiled faintly. "None of it was your fault. But why would someone want to shoot you?"

G.W. shook his head. "I don't have any idea."

He leaned back to look at Cole. "You fired anybody lately?"

Cole's dark brows arched into a frown. "Nope."

"Must have been a bushranger hoping to rob us. Cole's shot must have scared him off," G.W. murmured.

Rebecca checked his bandage, pleased to see the bleeding had stopped. "Do you think you could eat something? It would help keep up your strength," she said.

G.W. nodded. "I could eat if I had a pretty nurse to help me." He attempted to smile and winced with pain. He closed his eyes and gave in to his fatigue.

She patted his hand. "I'll be back with some food."

Cole followed her from the room. He laid his hand on her arm to detain her, saying, "It would help us if you could stay a few days and take care of him."

Rebecca bit her lip. "I've been anxious to get to the ranch, but I suppose a few days wouldn't hurt. I'd like to make sure he's going to be all right."

Cole felt his anger rise. "You're still planning to live at your ranch after what just happened?" His words spilled out explosively.

Rebecca stared into his intense, dark eyes and shivered. Why did he feel so strongly about her decision? The compassion she had sensed upon her arrival had evaporated when she announced her decision to stay. Was she so repugnant that he could not bear the thought of having her for a neighbor?

Rebecca straightened her shoulders. "I've told you all along what my plans are. I won't give up my father's ranch and I won't be forced into a marriage of convenience."

"Then you're a fool. I suppose you didn't learn anything by nearly getting G.W. killed."

Rebecca drew a sharp breath. The shock of his accusation struck her like a blow. "You're blaming me for what happened out there? I hardly see how it was my fault."

Cole hated himself for the harsh words. Still, he couldn't stop them. "G.W. wouldn't have been there if it weren't for you."

Rebecca narrowed her eyes. "I suppose next you'll blame me for the wagon accident that killed my father." Her voice was terse, yet tears filled her eyes.

A tense silence stretched between them. The muscles in Cole's jaw tightened as the color faded from his handsome face.

"No. I don't blame you for that." For a moment, a gloomy torment lay in his eyes. It was replaced by grim resignation as he turned away.

"I'd better see to the horses."

She watched the sag of his broad shoulders as he re-treated. She wanted to say something to bring him back, to make him explain why he disliked her. But she could think of nothing to say, so she let him go. His unfairness made her resolve to ignore his opinion.

She had always been strong-minded. Her aunt's harshest punishments had failed to break her will. She would run her father's ranch and she would do it as well as any man. And she wouldn't even consider marriage until she proved herself to Cole McBride and heard him admit that he'd been wrong about where she belonged.

Rebecca spent the next three days bringing food to G.W., changing his bandage, and sponging his brow on hot after-noons. The time she spent with him allowed their friendship to bloom. He was a patient and honorable man who did not complain about his discomfort and seemed truly grateful for her care. His amber eyes lit up each time she entered the room and followed her with a calf-like gaze as she moved about. She saw the longing that revealed his need for female companionship. He was moving toward middle age. He was settled and successful and yearned for a fam-ily. She understood. As a young girl she had dreamed of falling deeply and hopelessly in love. She'd been sure she would recognize her beloved when she looked into his eyes.

When she looked at G.W., she felt sympathy for his pain. She admired him. She enjoyed his company. Yet, when she lay in bed at night and tried to imagine herself becoming his wife, she found she could not.

If her aunt Abigail were here, Rebecca felt sure she would think her foolish. G.W. had a fine home, much nicer than the little shack her father had built. She shivered at the memory of her aunt's angry tirades, of how her dark eyes had flashed with anger each time she thumped the floor with her cane.

Rebecca drew a deep breath and tried to relax. It didn't

matter now. Abigail wasn't here and Rebecca was free to make her own decisions.

Under her careful nursing, G.W. passed out of danger and grew steadily better each day. At last, Rebecca decided to stay one more day and then head for Kangaroo Flats. She looked forward to leaving and escaping Cole's lingering disapproval. Though she saw little of him as he busied himself around the ranch, Rebecca sensed the wall he'd built between them. He acknowledged her with only a grudging nod when he popped in to check on G.W. and update him on ranch affairs. His unfairness hurt her. While he was with G.W. she would slip from the room and join Davies in the kitchen. In contrast to Cole, the good-natured brawny cook was only too happy to have her help with the endless duties of cooking for a large crew of men.

That night, Rebecca thumped her pillow in a vain effort to get comfortable. The room felt stuffy. There was no breeze to disturb the curtains. The chirping cicadas had ceased and the cackling kookaburra that G.W. had sent Davies to shoo out of the gum tree had grown quiet. Grasshoppers that sounded like hundreds of clocks being wound at once had replaced them.

In Sydney, Rebecca had longed for the familiar sounds of the outback. She'd found them comforting every night since her arrival. But tonight she couldn't sleep.

She threw back the sheet and rose from the bed. Wrapping her thin robe about her, she eased into the dark hall and headed for the door, careful not to brush against anything that would wake G.W.

She opened the door and stepped onto the porch. She needed fresh air and a view of the stars. Holding the porch rail, she leaned far out into the night, inhaling the myrtles' sweet fragrance.

Here, with the vast openness spread before her, she felt free. The stars blinked encouragement and the sounds of the dingoes beckoned her toward the freedom of the wild.

Rebecca tossed back her hair and closed her eyes, letting the faint breezes caress her cheek. Suddenly, instinct told her she was not alone. Frightened by the memory of G.W.'s attacker, she whirled and stared hard into the darkness.

Chapter three

Wally chuckled as Rebecca drew a sharp breath. The whites of his eyes contrasted sharply with the darkness, the moon illuminating his shadowy figure. Though he stood nearly beside her, she had never heard him coming.

Rebecca was sure he was proud of his stealth. The natives were like cats, moving silently in the dark. Over the years it had become a game to many of them. They prided themselves on their ability to appear seemingly out of nowhere and disappear just as quickly, scoring points when they took bushmen unaware.

"No fear, Missy. They call me Wally." His English was good, if halting.

The staccato beat of Rebecca's heart settled back to a steady rhythm. She squinted into the darkness, wondering if curiosity had led Wally to speak to her.

"I've seen you in the brush," she said.

"I work for Cole when he needs me. Other times I work for myself."

"You mean you work for G.W.," she corrected.

Wally shook his head. "G.W.'s a good man. But Cole's like a brother. He gives me sheep for work." Wally touched the spot above his heart and repeated, "I work for Cole."

28

Rebecca smiled, amused by his inability to grasp the concept of private property. In his culture, no one owned land. They merely borrowed it for food and shelter.

"You like Cole, then?" She didn't know why she should pursue the subject, but something urged her on.

Wally grinned, showing uneven rows of white teeth. "He's a good man."

Rebecca snorted in contempt. "He certainly doesn't like me."

Wally laughed softly. "He likes you much, too much."

The natives were frank with their opinions. It was one of the things Rebecca liked most about them. But she could not agree with his assessment.

She shook her head. "I don't think so."

Wally continued to chuckle. "Watch. You will see."

Rebecca's palms grew damp, and she wiped them along the hard split rail of the porch. She had thought Cole had written her off as a foolish woman. Now, Wally's strange comment threw her heart into confusion. She turned to ask why he was so sure, but he had slipped away as quietly as he had appeared. She dismissed Wally's insight as the musing of an active imagination.

A chill crept into the air. Rebecca shivered as she slipped quietly into the house and slid back into bed. She pulled the covers snugly above her, wishing they could protect her from the confusion that engulfed her.

She envisioned G.W.'s round face and frowned. As much as she admired him, she could not make herself desire him. She blushed at her bold admission—even as she wondered if, perhaps, she should not indulge herself by insisting on the sort of romance she had envisioned as a schoolgirl.

She twisted under the blankets as doubts plagued her. Her life felt as uncharted as the distant outback. If only something good could come of her return, it might someday fill the void left by her father's death.

She drifted to sleep with the determination to be patient.

Rebecca awoke late and scurried to dress. Every day since G.W. was shot, she had brought him breakfast in bed. She knew he looked forward to her presence.

Today, she found his room empty, his covers pulled untidily across his bed. She scurried down the hall, intending to check the kitchen.

When Davies stepped out of the kitchen, carrying a tray, Rebecca nearly collided with him. She gave a small gasp of surprise. "I was looking for G.W."

Davies nodded toward the front porch. His swarthy face broke into a grin. "He had me help him up. He thought you might like to join him for breakfast on the porch."

Rebecca frowned. She couldn't help wondering if G.W.'s decision to spend a romantic morning with her would hamper his recovery. "Are you sure it's not too soon?"

"G.W.'s tough as they come, 'cept maybe for Cole," he added thoughtfully. He shook his shaggy head. "It'll take more than a bullet to keep the boss down."

She smiled. "I guess you're right. He's been getting stronger every day."

She followed Davies to the front veranda, where the sunshine soaked into her body and soul. It slanted across the weathered boards, lighting the spot where she'd stood with Wally last night. She shivered as she remembered their strange conversation. Then she turned her attention to G.W. "So, you were ready for a little fresh air?"

He smiled. She was pleased to see the rosy color restored to his face. The worn blanket wrapped across his shoulders was the only hint that he had been injured.

Davies set the tray of biscuits and scrambled eggs on a chair next to G.W. Steam rose from the hot food and evaporated in the mild chill of the air. The familiar aroma of breakfast awakened Rebecca's stomach as she accepted a mug of coffee. It was strong and hot and left a slightly acrid taste in her mouth. It took something this strong to satisfy a crowd of tough ranch hands.

Davies left Rebecca in charge of the food and returned to the kitchen. She knew a passel of pans and dishes awaited him from the early breakfast he'd fixed for the hands.

She handed G.W. a plate of eggs and biscuits. "I hope you haven't waited for your breakfast too long. I slept later than I intended. If I stayed here any longer I'd get comfortably lazy."

"I'm glad you're comfortable here." G.W. leaned forward. His eyes were earnest amber orbs. "I'd love to keep you safe and spoil you as much as you'd allow."

Rebecca felt her eyes grow misty. "I know you would. You are one of the sweetest men I've ever met. I'm glad I got to know you better."

Rebecca saw the lump rise and fall in his throat as G.W. swallowed hard. "I know we could be happy, Rebecca. If you marry me, you won't have to give up Kangaroo Flats. We could make it part of this ranch."

"It's a generous offer. I'll think about it."

G.W. sat back in the chair and took a sip of coffee. "It's not good to be alone in this country. I don't want anything to happen to you."

She patted his hand. "I'll be careful."

G.W. nodded. "I hope you're right. Consider my offer, though. It's open any time."

"I will. Unless you find someone else and take it back." Rebecca grinned mischievously.

"I don't think you'll have much competition out here." He waved his left hand toward the vast expanse of land. No appearance of life, man or animal, existed in sunlight or shadows. Yet the seeming emptiness was contradicted by the sounds surrounding them. The ebb and flow of cicadas, primordial as the ocean, blended with the voices of birds of every kind in a cacophony of squawk and song.

G.W. shifted in the rocker hand-carved by his father. The chair creaked under his weight. He took a sip of coffee, brows puckering in thought as he said, "I've lived all my life out here. I've never had a chance to go courting. So, I've had to be patient and wait for a woman to come into my life. I do not believe that the circumstances that put us together happened by chance."

He wore the expression of a checker player considering his next move. He was used to taking charge—he had tamed a wilderness to suit his needs. With nature, hard work yielded desired results. Yet he knew that dealing with women called for a different approach. He couldn't win her heart by sheer force.

He smiled at her. "I suppose waiting a little longer will not do me any harm. Would you mind if I called on you once in a while when you get home?" A flame of hope burned in his amber eyes.

She nodded thoughtfully. "I'd welcome the company. I'm sure I'll get lonely. Perhaps you could bring a book from the library I saw in your sitting room and we could read together."

She saw expectancy light his face. "I don't read well, but it would be a pleasure for me to listen to you."

"Then it's settled. As soon as you're well you can come and stay for supper."

He grinned. "How about Saturday? Each Saturday night."

Rebecca admired the simple joy that showed on the round, genial face. She wondered with a pang of guilt why she could not muster romantic feelings for this man. Her father had wanted it. And it made sense. They could join the two ranches. Still, she knew the heart did not follow logic's rules.

"Each Saturday evening," she agreed.

"I can hardly wait. I suppose you'll be leaving in a little while."

She nodded. "I have my things packed. I'm ready any time."

She reached into her pocket and withdrew a slender, folded piece of paper. "Do you suppose someone could deliver this letter on the next trip to Bathurst? It is to a woman I met on the stage."

G.W. accepted it, letting his fingers graze her warm hand. "I would be happy to send it along."

Rebecca smiled gratefully. "And do you suppose I could borrow a horse? I'll take good care of it until you can fetch it back."

G.W. acknowledged her request with a frown. "I won't let you go alone."

His condescension galled her. "I know my way back. Surely you don't think in your weakened condition . . ."

He held up his hand to stop her. "I admit I'm not up to the ride just yet. But whoever took a shot at me might still be out there. I'm not asking you for any more than to give me a little peace of mind. Let me send Cole with you."

She caught her lip in her teeth as her heart gave a painful thump. She would rather he'd suggested any guardian but the stern, disapproving foreman. But how could she protest? G.W. had shown her such kindness upon her arrival that she owed him a gracious parting.

She forced a smile. "I hope you can forgive me. Everybody wants to protect me and I have been looking forward to independence. But it's no excuse for rudeness. I'd be glad to accept Cole's escort if that would ease your mind."

G.W. shifted, guiding his injured arm into a more comfortable position. "It would ease my mind. I only wish I could see to you personally."

Suddenly Rebecca remembered that Cole had sent Wally to track the assailant. "Did Wally find the tracks of the man who shot you?"

G.W. pursed his lips into a thin line. "He did. The tracks

led to Andrew Finley's property. That no-good squatter probably hired someone to take a shot at me."

"Why?"

G.W. gave a harsh laugh. "He probably thought he'd expand his ranch by getting me out of the way. He'd slit his own grandmother's throat if he thought he could make a profit. You watch out for him. Your little ranch sits on the best portion of the creek."

Rebecca's spine prickled. "He wasn't here when I left ten years ago."

"No. He came right after you left. He's been a curse to the whole range. He steals sheep and I believe he killed two of my bushmen, though I can't prove it."

Rebecca stared into the perfect sunlit day. She loved this land. The memories of it had sustained her during her troubles in Sydney. Yet she was realistic about the dangers that lurked for the unwary. Her father had taught her to be alert to the daily threat of snakes and funnel-web spiders, dehydration and heat exhaustion. She could deal with those.

A human opponent posed a different sort of threat. No matter how careful she might be, she could not protect herself from an enemy who was determined and ruthless. Nor did she have G.W.'s resources. He could lose a hundred sheep and not suffer financial ruin. She could not.

A warm breeze ruffled her hair, bringing the scent of horses and wildflowers, chickens and strong lye soap that Davies used in the kitchen. They were the comforting smells of spring she remembered from home.

Surely the warning G.W. had planted in her mind was well-intentioned but unnecessary. She would mind her own business, staying clear of Andrew Finley. And he would stay clear of her. She would be content, except for missing her father. And life would be good. She'd spent too long yearning to come home to accept anything less.

* * *

Cole finished assisting with a difficult lambing and looked over the sheep. They stretched as far as his eye could see, scattered about like balls of cotton. Soon he would be busy with shearing.

He was glad for the distraction of hard work. Even so, it took an effort to keep his mind off Rebecca. And he did not often succeed. In fact, he spent so much time congratulating himself about putting her out of his mind that he finally had to admit to himself that he wasn't likely to ever forget her. Her delicate face was etched in his memory. He would always remember how she looked standing in the street the first day they met, lost and vulnerable.

His heart ached with the recollection. He had avoided her while she stayed at the ranch tending to G.W. He hoped that if he avoided her long enough he could forget the mixture of guilt and admiration she evoked in him. He could not let himself care too much about her welfare. He had decided long ago that life was too harsh to care too much for anyone. He had learned from hard experience the pain of failing to protect a loved one and losing them.

As he ran a hand along a sheep's leg, inspecting a small cut, his thoughts strayed unwillingly to his painful past. How he had hated Andrew Finley, who had moved them here then turned on them like a monster. The memory of his mother brought an ache to his heart. If he had been older, he could have stopped the mental and physical abuse that led to her early death. But he had been only a child, unable to defend himself from the same mistreatment.

Cole stared across the miles that separated him from his old home. If G.W. had not hired him and taken him in, he felt sure either he or his stepfather would be dead.

He felt the warm sun across his back and drew in a deep breath of wildflowers and sheep. Life was good here. He witnessed no angry beatings or berating words. G.W. was not only an employer who had saved him from destruction, he was also a trusted friend.

The fact that someone had tried to kill him filled Cole with suspicion. If the man who had shot G.W. had come from Finley's ranch, Finley had surely had a hand in the act.

Cole puzzled over the possible motives while he finished bandaging the legs of several sheep that had been rescued from a band of dingoes. Though Cole did not doubt that Finley coveted G.W.'s ranch, he'd never been bold enough to attempt to take it. But if Finley set his mind to something, he was as deadly as a death adder.

The cackle of kookaburras from their homes in the gum trees filled the air. The disparity between his mood and the birds' noisy laughter set his nerves on edge. Cole's hair prickled on the back of his neck as he scanned the open grassland. A premonition of danger gripped him.

He wiped his damp brow and glanced at the men who were busy finishing the various custodial chores with the sheep. Soon, half the group would return to the house for lunch and new chore assignments. The other half would stay with the sheep, guarding them until time to round them up.

Cole planned to spend the afternoon doing repairs on the sheds. He was glad for an excuse to stick close to the house. Though it would be hard for a gunman to sneak all the way to the residence without being noticed, Cole worried about G.W. and he wanted to keep watch.

His apprehension subsided when he reached the back steps of the kitchen and smelled the familiar beans and bread that Davies was setting out for lunch. His stomach crawled with hunger. He'd been working hard since daybreak. Perhaps hunger and fatigue had contributed to his feeling of doom. He'd feel better once he ate.

He found Davies in the kitchen. The cook held a monstrous cast iron pot in one brawny arm while dishing beans onto chipped china plates.

"How's the boss?" Cole asked.

Davies grinned, his tongue protruding through a gap in his teeth. "He felt good enough to take breakfast on the porch with the lady. He'll be back on his horse in a few days."

Cole knew Davies held G.W. in high esteem. The ex-convict had suffered ill treatment before being taken in by G.W., and would give his life for his boss if need be.

The other men joined them in the kitchen, talking and washing down bread with bountiful mugs of coffee. Cole finished his last swig of the brew and stood, preparing to head for the barn, when Davies said, "Boss wants to see you when you're done. He's restin' in his room."

Cole headed to the bedroom, expecting G.W. to want a report of the morning's work. The door stood open. Cole knocked lightly on the frame and entered at G.W.'s invitation.

Rebecca sat in a chair near the bed. She glanced up, her creamy cheeks coloring slightly as Cole nodded a greeting.

"Davies said you wanted to see me."

G.W. nodded. He had not shaved since the morning he was shot. Light from the window lit the red stubble that was growing into a scraggly beard. "Rebecca is moving to her ranch this afternoon. I want you to see she gets there safe."

Cole sensed that Rebecca was watching him. He avoided her eyes. "I was fixin' to start repairs. Maybe one of the other hands . . ."

G.W. cut him short. "I don't trust the other hands. Set somebody else to work on the barn and hitch up the wagon."

G.W.'s order did not coincide with Cole's plan to avoid Rebecca. He wanted to protest, to insist on remaining at the ranch. Yet what reason could he give?

Stuck with the task, he decided to complete it as soon as possible. "I'll get the horses. That all you wanted to see me about?"

"That's all."

Cole nodded curtly and strode from the room.

Rebecca watched him go. She unclasped her fingers, only to recapture them in a fruitless gesture. "I don't think your foreman likes me very much," she remarked.

G.W.'s brow puckered. "Cole's not the social type. When the other men go into town for fun, Cole stays behind and takes a trek with Wally or just sits and whittles. It's like he's got something on his mind that won't let him loose. Don't take it personal."

"I won't." She stood to take leave. "I'll be forever grateful for your kindness when I arrived here."

G.W.'s broad face colored pleasurably. "The enjoyment was mine, I'm only sorry for the circumstances that made it necessary."

Rebecca reached down and gently squeezed his hand. "Thank you. I'll look forward to your Saturday visits. Just be sure you're really up to it before you make the trip." She waited on the porch as Cole halted the wagon. Without a word, he took her bags and swung them onto the seat.

Rebecca watched him with mounting discomfort. She disliked being a burden, especially to a man whose broad shoulders and lean build attracted her in spite of herself.

She paused beside the wagon. "I don't want to put you to trouble. I'm sure I could get back with the loan of a horse."

"I was told to escort you."

His sharp answer stung her, bringing tears to her eyes. She jerked her elbow out of his grasp as he helped her into the wagon. She set her gaze stonily ahead, determined to endure his company for G.W.'s sake. If she wasn't concerned with G.W.'s peace of mind, she would climb from the wagon and walk home.

Rebecca's rebuff caused Cole to grimace with remorse. He could not tell her that his hardness was the only protection he held against her charms. Dropping this protection would cast him into a sinkhole from which he could never escape; she reminded him of something he would prefer to forget.

He climbed beside her and grimly took the reins. It was better for her to think him churlish than to begin a friendship that had no future. He had learned long ago not to waste effort pursuing things he could never have. And he felt sure he could never have more than a passing acquaintance with Rebecca Dalton.

Chapter four

The silence between Rebecca and Cole was an uncomfortable contrast to the opera of insects and birds as the wagon cut across the endless waves of grass. The relentless heat made Rebecca's dress stick to her body. The air hung still and heavy. It would be hours before she could expect the relief of a cooling breeze.

She was aware of Cole's every movement as he sat beside her. His hands moved to the rhythm of the reins, and his body swayed slightly to the movement of the wagon. He reminded her of a stallion her father had showed her long ago, which had once belonged to an officer who had supervised convicts building the road through the Blue Mountains. The officer had been murdered and his horse had gone wild.

The spirited creature roamed the grasslands. His chestnut coat gleamed in the sun and his streaming mane flowed wildly as he came and went where he pleased. When Rebecca had asked about taming him, her father had shaken his head. "He's wonderful to look at, but he's been away from people too long. Anyone who gets close to him is likely to get hurt."

Even so, she had lain awake at night imagining herself

40

the only one able to tame the beast. She had dreamed of riding him across the meadows, admired by everyone who saw them.

Rebecca smiled at the childish memory of how she'd planned to offer sugar to the horse and how he'd nibble it gently from her fingers. But she'd never ever gotten close to the horse. She was not likely to get close to Cole either.

To keep him from her mind, she studied the scenery. They passed under a large gum tree and she smiled at the sight of a koala stretched lazily across a branch. His dark eyes squinted at them. He seemed annoyed at having his sleep disturbed.

A kangaroo looked up from grazing and Rebecca noticed a tiny head poking out from the pouch. These familiar scenes from childhood tugged at her heart with bittersweet memories. Her father, too, had loved this land and every animal in it. Now she was going home, but home would not be the same. The last time she had lived here had been with her mother and father. Now both of them were gone. How would she feel when she stepped through the door and saw the familiar furniture but not the two familiar faces from her childhood?

At least Ned was still there. It would be good to see Ned.

Cole's voice startled her from her thoughts. "I'm sorry we couldn't have started earlier in the morning when it wasn't so hot."

She glanced at him, expecting him to show contempt for her frailty. Instead, she saw honest concern that recalled the gentleness he had shown when they first met.

She bit back a sharp answer and said simply, "I'm used to the heat. It doesn't bother me."

Cole's jaw flinched as he turned his attention back to the wagon. She studied him for a moment, wondering what qualities lurked under his strong exterior. Perhaps there was a way through the cold disapproval after all.

Her heartbeat quickened with the challenge. She had no

desire to complete this trip in silence. But he had become taciturn again. Would he respond to her attempt at conversation?

She drew a deep breath, determined to try. "It will be strange to be home after being away so long. I'm sure my father changed over the years, though I still imagined him looking like he did when I was a little girl."

She paused, wondering if he were listening. "And Ned wasn't a young man when I left. I'm sure he's changed. And surely the house is a bit worse for wear, with two bachelors living there these last eight years."

Sucking in her breath, she wondered if Cole would respond. The seconds ticked by. His eyes roved the landscape as though he expected danger from any direction.

Rebecca had almost given up hope of an answer when Cole said, "Time changes everything, sometimes for better. Sometimes for worse. I'm sure the house is more weatherworn than you remember. If we'd had time to write to you about your father, you could have stayed comfortably in Sydney."

"That's not true. I was never comfortable there. I lived with my aunt and home was never happy."

Cole's head jerked toward her as though she'd pulled a string. For a moment their eyes met, and she saw his confusion and pain.

"What was this aunt like?" he asked.

"Cruel." Rebecca sighed. "I don't think she meant to be cruel, but I was only a child and her standards were too high. She expected me to work like an adult and punished my childish silliness with a switch."

She saw his mouth tighten. His hands tensed on the reins. He licked dry lips and said, "Some people use kids as slaves."

"That's true, though my aunt merely considered it discipline. My mother was a spoiled woman who liked her gin. Perhaps my aunt didn't want me to turn out like her."

He scowled. "Beatings don't convince most people how much you care."

"Of course not. When I think back, though, I believe the criticism was harder to bear than the whippings. Sometimes I felt so worthless, the only thing that got me up in the morning was the fear of my aunt's wrath. I would have slid completely into depression if I had not believed I would escape someday."

"It seems both our mothers made bad decisions," Cole said grimly.

"What did your mother decide?" Rebecca asked timidly.

"She was a widow and I was young. She came out here and married a squatter who mistreated her from the day she arrived."

And you too?"

"Me too. I know what it's like to be beaten for the slightest thing and what it's like to be told you're worthless. I lived that way until I was rescued by G.W. Sanders."

Rebecca felt as though blinders had been pulled from her eyes. It wasn't her recollections of childhood that produced such an intense reaction in Cole. It was his own deep pain.

A heavy silence grew as Cole fought to exhibit a composure he didn't feel. He admired Rebecca for forging out from Sydney and escaping her aunt's tyranny. Hadn't he done the same thing when he decided he could no longer abide life under Finley's roof?

He gripped the reins tighter as his frustration grew. He wondered if Rebecca understood the risk she took in thinking that her lot here would prove easier than life in Sydney. His mother had believed the same thing and had been sadly mistaken. She had once been young and pretty, just like Rebecca. She had come here to make a home. Yet she'd suffered only hardship and abuse. He couldn't bear to think of Rebecca growing old before her time, slaving to manage both her homestead and her sheep.

Ned was getting old. He wouldn't be able to manage

even her small ranch forever. What then? Would she labor side by side in the hot sun with rough and sometimes dangerous hired men?

He had a notion to take her right back to G.W. He was a good man who could give her the protection she deserved. And G.W. wanted Rebecca. She would fill the void of loneliness he had borne for so many years. If a wedding was in the cards, Cole would attend and offer his congratulations. His loyalty to G.W. was without question. Yet, deep in his heart, Cole knew he was glad Rebecca had tabled G.W.'s offer.

This knowledge pricked at his conscience. He should be glad for G.W.'s happiness. It would be more good fortune than most men deserved to have a spirited woman like Rebecca for a life partner. Maybe someday, when she was safely married to G.W., he would face her with the truth. It would be painful if Rebecca could not forgive him for his part in causing her father's death. Still, he could not bear to carry his guilty secret to his grave. He had been too much of a coward to tell Rebecca the truth when she arrived, to confess how the accident had been his fault. The accusation drummed in his mind to the beat of the horses' hooves as they came in sight of the house.

He sensed Rebecca's mounting tension. Eight years was a long time to be parted from the home she loved.

He pulled the wagon into the yard, stirring up a thick cloud of dust. The house looked deserted, as did the small lean-to where Ned lived.

Rebecca climbed from the wagon and coughed in the settling dust. Even though she'd seen his grave, she half-expected her father to come through the door, arms open wide to greet her. She blinked back tears as she wiped her hand across her cheek. It felt gritty from moisture and dust. She didn't have her father, but she was home. She had always known she would come back. This was her destiny and she would build a life here.

She stared at the tiny cottage, letting reality replace memory. The acacia wood had weathered, but all the boards were still nailed neatly in place. Repairs had kept the roof tightly thatched. Except for the railed front porch, the house was still shaped like a box, square with four interior rooms of equal size. Rebecca remembered each of them as though she had just stepped outside for a moment.

She was barely aware that Cole had joined her, holding her travel bags in hand. She walked slowly up the porch steps, noticing one that had been recently replaced with newer, lighter wood. It was her father's nature to be a good steward. He would not have given in to despair and let his home suffer when her mother left. In the back of his mind, she was sure he held the hope they would join him one day and find the home they had left worthy of their return.

A goanna moved lazily away from them. Rebecca saw the lizard's tail disappear beneath the far rail and was glad they had not taken it by surprise. She remembered a scar her father carried on his arm from an accidental encounter.

She climbed the two sturdy steps, feeling uncertain about facing the memories waiting inside. She reminded herself that this was her home as she pushed open the front door. The quiet darkness greeted her. It felt empty and impersonal.

She bit her lip as she stepped into the parlor. The flowered settee that her parents had brought from Sydney still sat against the near wall. The coffee table her father had crafted from acacia still held the family Bible.

She imagined her father reading from it each night as he had done when she was a child. Her mother sat next to him, hardly seeming to hear the words as she completed the endless task of mending clothes that grew threadbare much too quickly in rough country. Rebecca could hear her father's deep, animated voice.

Fighting back tears, she turned to inspect the kitchen. Her father had managed well on his own. Dishes were stacked neatly on the small shelf he had built. Pans were washed and hung on their hooks. The table held a bowl of wildflowers that were beginning to show signs of wilting.

"I bet those were for me," she said, her voice shaky as she nodded toward the flowers. Cole gripped the bags tightly and wondered if she expected a reply. He wished there were something he could say to ease this bittersweet homecoming. Rebecca looked so pure and beautiful, he longed to touch her face and gently wipe away the tears that clung to her lashes. He resisted the urge, sure she would misinterpret his intention.

After a moment she glanced at him. "I've left you standing here wondering what to do with my bags. My room is down the hall." Her lips quivered as she attempted to regain her composure.

She walked down the central hall that divided each side of the house and paused at the doorway on the right. "My old room. It looks just like the day I left."

Cole set down the bags. As he watched her walk into her room, he understood how a home could be filled with good memories and love. For the briefest of moments, he imagined himself on his own homestead, sharing life with a wife like Rebecca, loving and being loved in return. Sunlight fell in a shaft, bathing her in light. Cole wondered what it would feel like to hold a woman he loved and stroke her silky hair, to embrace her and tell her he would never let anything hurt her again. He swallowed hard, reminding himself that he dared have no such dreams. He was a hired hand. What could he offer a woman?

The front door creaked on its hinges, and then swung closed with a soft thud. Cole tensed, reaching instinctively for his gun as Rebecca turned expectantly toward the sound.

A man's voice called from the sitting room.

Rebecca rushed past Cole. He followed and saw her father's trusted old foreman, who was blinking at the sight of her. She flew toward him and grasped his hand, crying, "Ned! I'm so glad you're still here."

Despite his years, Ned's eyes were still bright blue. His face, creased and browned as a walnut, regarded her with a fatherly kindness. "Rebecca, lass, how you've changed over the years. I always knew you'd grow into a beauty. It's good to have you back."

Rebecca let his strong accent wash over her like the soft water of a warm bath. Blushing at his compliment, she said, "I'm glad to be back."

She lowered her eyes. "I still can't believe my father is gone. I know you miss him as much as I do."

The small man stood at eye level with Rebecca. He regarded her a moment, then said softly, "My saddest day was burying your father. He was the best friend I ever had."

Rebecca searched his face, finding comfort in their shared loss. "He thought highly of you, too."

Ned nodded. "I want you to know that he died a happy man. Knowing you were finally coming home meant everything to him. The day before the accident, he cleaned this whole place."

Rebecca felt new tears sting her eyes. She was glad when Ned turned his attention to Cole and said, "The wagon was busted up pretty good, but I fixed it solid. It's hard to run a sheep station without a good wagon. I hope ye don't mind I didn't ask ye to fix it."

Cole's jaw tensed. "No reason I should mind. I have plenty to do to keep me busy."

"Why didn't G.W. bring the lass?"

Rebecca broke in. "G.W. was shot in the shoulder when he took me to see Father's grave. I've been there a few days tending to his wound."

"Shot? By who?"

Rebecca shrugged. "He thinks a man named Andrew Finley hired someone."

"Probably right. How did this man know ye'd be out at the grave?"

"I don't know. He must have been watching for us."

Ned fell silent. Cole felt his narrowed gaze and burned with a cold fury at the accusation in Ned's eyes. He knew the old man didn't trust him. Ned thought Cole had dealings with Finley. The thought turned Cole's stomach. If Andrew Finley were caught in a bushfire, Cole wouldn't lift a finger to help him. Cole set his jaw, meeting the old man's eyes with his own dark anger.

He wondered if anyone else questioned his loyalty. He was sure of G.W.'s trust in him. But he wondered about the men who worked beside him. Some of them knew about his connection to Finley. Maybe some of them worried he'd pitch in with the squatter to put a bullet in their backs.

If only someone would say it to his face, he could use words, fists, or whatever was necessary to defend himself against the accusations. Instead, subtle hints chased him until he felt like an insect caught in a spider's web, still alive, yet condemned.

A glance at Rebecca caused him to wince. Her smooth forehead puckered into a frown as though she sensed the animosity between the two men.

What a fool he had been for allowing himself to indulge in their shared childhood misfortunes. He guessed that when he left, Ned would share his suspicions. After that, Rebecca would never look at him without despising him.

He stooped to retrieve the hat he'd tossed near the open door. "I'd best be getting back."

He thought he caught a flash of disappointment in Rebecca's clear blue eyes as she rushed to say, "I was hoping to pay you for some of your trouble by cooking your supper. I don't know what's in the kitchen but I'm sure there's something to make a meal."

He hesitated, drawn by the sincerity of her invitation. He wanted to listen to the soft cadence of her voice while she reminisced about her past. And though it was inevitable that she would come to hate him, perhaps he could put it off a little longer by staying for dinner.

He nodded in answer. "I'd be pleased to stay, but not because you owe me anything."

She watched him with a steady gaze. He imagined she could read the guilt in his eyes. He expected her to change her mind and send him away.

Instead, she smiled. "I'll see what's in the kitchen."

She turned to Ned. "Is there flour for biscuits?"

The old man nodded, frowning at the prospect of sharing them with Cole. "There's also fresh lamb. I cured it yesterday."

Rebecca nodded briskly, relieved to have a duty to occupy her attention. "I'll begin supper. You can visit with Cole if you like."

"I still have to tend to the animals. I came in because I saw the wagon," Ned said.

Rebecca was already heading for the kitchen. "Supper should be done by the time you finish."

Cole rolled up his sleeves and followed her. "I'll help if you tell me what to do."

She turned with a shy smile. "On Sundays, my father used to help my mother in the kitchen. Then he'd joke about whether we should eat what he'd cooked."

Cole watched her tie a towel around her slender waist.

Rebecca glanced at him, discovering an unreadable expression in his eyes. She was suddenly aware of the comparison she had made between her parents and the two strangers now alone in the kitchen. She flushed. Would he think her simple comment forward?

Lowering her eyes, she said, "If you like, you can light the stove while I find a pan."

Cole had the stove ready when she finished laying lamb steaks in the pan to fry. While she cut biscuit dough with a tin cup, she watched Cole set the table and turn the steaks.

She stared admiringly at his broad shoulders and strong hands as he arranged mismatched mugs and plates on the table. For a tall man, he moved about the kitchen with ease.

He glanced up to see her staring and she looked down quickly, feeling as though she'd been caught with her thoughts written on her face. Fumbling, she opened the oven and shoved the pan of biscuits inside. A quick turn to get a platter for the steaks ran her squarely into Cole's solid chest. She stepped back with a squeak of surprise, feeling the heat of the oven uncomfortably warm against the back of her legs.

Cole offered her the platter. "I must have read your mind. I was thinking the steaks would be done."

She looked into his dark eyes and felt a shiver run the length of her spine. She could not deny the attraction of his strong chin, slender nose, and wavy dark hair that brushed the collar of a shirt that lay open at the neck. There was something a little untamed about him. Yet when she looked into his eyes, she saw a plea to fill a need she could not identify.

Recovering her senses, Rebecca took the platter. "Everything should be ready as soon as Ned comes in."

As she lifted the steaks from the pan, she sensed Cole's eyes following every movement she made.

The food sat steaming on the table when Ned came in, hands still wet from washing at the trough. They sat down together and Ned stabbed a solid bite of meat. Before he popped it into his mouth he told Rebecca, "Ye'll have plenty of time to catch up on the news around here. Now, tell us what ye've been doing for the last eight years."

Rebecca found herself doing most of the talking. Not until they had finished eating did talk drift to plans for the ranch. Cole asked Ned if he intended to tie onto the fence he had been building to keep dingoes away from the sheep.

Ned shook his head. " 'Tis too big a project for me, with shearing season coming on."

Ned sat back in his chair and wiped greasy fingers across his pants. "Is Andrew tying on?"

Rebecca sensed the tension between the men. Their eyes locked in a long, cold stare. Cole's rigid bearing reminded her of a tight spring, ready to explode at the slightest provocation.

He pushed back in his chair. "I haven't offered to let him."

He glanced at Rebecca, who bit her lip at the chill in his eyes. "I've got to get back. Thank you for the meal." His words were formal, his back stiff as he rose.

Rebecca scrambled to her feet. "Thank you for taking the trouble to see me home."

Cole nodded, avoiding another look at Ned. "My pleasure. I can see myself out," he added abruptly.

Rebecca hesitated, uncertain whether to follow him. At last, she followed slowly and watched him retrieve his hat. His head barely cleared the door frame as he disappeared into the evening light.

He swung onto his bay and nudged her into a canter, slowing a little as he put distance between himself and the shack. If only it would be as easy to escape from his desire to earn the good opinion of the woman inside. He gripped the reins and stared into the darkness, feeling as desolate as the vast bush land that filled his view.

Chapter five

Rebecca lingered in the doorway until Cole rode out of sight. The kitchen duties they had shared and his presence at her table had left her with a depth of yearning she was powerless to quench. What would it be like to have a man for whom she could cook and mend and raise a family?

She bit her lip, alarmed at the bottomless well of feeling such thoughts evoked. It was a girlish attraction to a handsome man and she needed to forget about it at once. It was pointless to allow herself to be drawn to a man who thought her a fool . . . would send her back to Sydney if he could.

A skillet clattered, telling her Ned had begun clearing the dishes. She hurried back to take on the task, a guilty flush warming her cheeks.

Ned had rolled back his sleeves to scrape the meat bones into the bucket beside the dish tub. Though he had always set great stock in minding his own business, his frown left no doubt that Rebecca had correctly read the disapproval in his faded blue eyes. She sensed he felt the need to impart advice, or perhaps a warning.

"Varmints don't change their nature by being set in a new place. An adder is just as deadly nesting on G.W.'s land or Andrew Finley's."

Exactly what he was trying to say escaped her comprehension. "I don't know what you're getting at," Rebecca said.

Ned's heavy brows furrowed into a deeper frown. "I don't like to discredit a man's character, but it's a fact that Cole was raised by Andrew Finley, the meanest snake that crawls the range. Even though he works for G.W. now, it doesn't mean he and Finley wouldn't like to get their hands on this land. The stretch of broad creek that crosses yer land narrows when it reaches Finley's place."

Rebecca struggled to make sense of the new information and how it affected her. She watched Ned's gnarled hands as he rubbed soap across the heavy skillet. Finally, she asked, "How could he get his hands on this ranch?"

Ned raised his brows. "Seems to me there's two ways, either murder or marriage."

Rebecca considered the two possibilities. Cole had not given her reason to believe he wished to court her. In fact, he had wanted to send her back to the city.

That left murder. Was Ned suggesting that Cole was capable of such a thing? Her mind refused to accept the possibility. She remembered the aborigine Wally joining her on the porch. Hadn't he said that Cole was a good man?

She shook her head, feeling her heart jump to Cole's defense. "If Finley was the man who married Cole's mother, then Cole holds him no loyalty. Cole told me the man mistreated the both of them."

Ned scowled. "Finley has a way of making people do what he wants."

Not Cole, she thought. She remembered the stubborn set of his chin and the anger that sparked in his eyes when he spoke of his mother's hardship. Unless he was a good liar, she felt sure that Cole was not in Andrew Finley's pocket.

Ned moved aside to let Rebecca settle the plates in the wash water. She still sensed his disapproval.

"Remember what I'm telling ye. I saw the way ye looked

at young Cole. Yer father's not here now to watch for ye, so I've got to speak my piece."

Rebecca felt her cheeks flush warm again. If her attraction to Cole was obvious to Ned, wasn't it equally obvious to Cole?

The old bushman reached for a wet plate and began to dry it with a fresh linen hand towel that Rebecca remembered seeing her mother embroider.

"Yer father hoped, once the two of ye had time to get reacquainted, ye'd want to marry G.W. Roger and I planned to stay here and run this place until we got too old. It wouldn't do Finley any good to kill us because the ranch would just go to G.W. As it is now . . ." He rubbed his grizzled chin as his words trailed off.

A shiver crept up Rebecca's spine. "You think we're really in danger?"

"Like I said, Finley has a way of getting what he wants. The only reason I'm still alive is that killing me wouldn't get him the ranch."

He rubbed his grizzled chin. "But ye, lass, hold the key."

Ned's words stuck in Rebecca's mind as she prepared for bed. She sat on a stool beside the window and looked into the sky. A lone mosquito buzzed near her face. Most shacks like this one had oilcloths that could be rolled down at night to keep out the insects. But oilcloth let in very little breeze. Her father had put in a fine mesh screen to ready the house for her arrival. No doubt the mesh had cost him dearly.

Her eyes filled with tears as she realized how willing he had always been to sacrifice for her comfort. Now, when she had a chance to marry G.W. and see to the security of her father's land, she could not force herself to comply. Instead, she had seemingly chosen to put herself and Ned in danger, something her father would never have wished.

If only he were here so she could explain her feelings.

She would tell him how she longed to marry for love. He had treated her mother with such tender thoughtfulness that she felt sure he had possessed a romantic heart.

Rebecca sighed as she reminded herself what bitter disappointment he had endured. Perhaps he would tell her that love was a silly notion. He had loved her mother, only to lose her to the lure of the city. Love was not the most practical reason for marriage.

She squeezed her eyes closed, determined to shut out the doubts and insecurities. Perhaps she would come to love G.W. after he came to visit each week. Loneliness did strange things to the heart. And she was sure to be lonely.

She slipped into bed and thumped her goosedown pillow into a hard knot. Although she tried to sleep, she was discomfited by the knowledge that no matter what seemed best for the ranch, she could not seem to control her stubborn heart.

Dawn painted pink swirls in the sky as Rebecca awoke from a dream about Abigail. The old woman had shaken her finger in Rebecca's face and threatened to disinherit her if she refused to marry G.W. In spite of the unsettling dream, the idea of Abigail sharing anything with her was so ludicrous that it made her smile.

She heard a pan clatter in the kitchen and knew Ned had already begun preparing breakfast. Snatching her faded blue calico from a hook, she hurriedly smoothed her hair into a loose chignon. Would Ned be receptive to her plans to work alongside him to inspect and tend the sheep?

Thin mutton steaks sizzled in the pan while Rebecca sliced leftover biscuits. Ned continued to stir the emu egg they would share after she announced her intention to accompany him. If he disapproved, his face did not betray him.

He nodded slowly. "Unless ye changed since ye were a wee lass, I didn't figure ye'd be content to stay in the house

and cook. Ye never had much interest in household things."
His voice held no criticism, just fact.

Rebecca cast him a sidelong look. "I'd be a terrible wife,
don't you think? I'd always want to be helping on the land.
And I'd neglect the house terribly."

Ned fixed her with a steady gaze. "Depends on what a
man wants, I guess. Yer father would have been happy with
a woman who showed interest in the ranch instead of running off to Sydney."

It was true. Her father had never minded Rebecca's wan-
derings about the ranch and the wild creatures she brought
home as pets. Her mother had thoroughly disapproved and
Abigail had been horrified at her upbringing. Yet there had
been nothing either woman could do to erase Rebecca's
love of this untamed land.

Ned saddled his bay and a roan for Rebecca. As the
mellow breeze carried the whispering of the grasses, Rebecca studied the breadth of the land she now owned.

She shrank from the idea of a quick marriage to relieve
her of responsibility for the ranch. Instead, she would dog
Ned's steps, paying careful attention to all he could teach
her. Then, when he became too old to work, she would be
capable of taking over the daily operations. And she would
be able to do it well.

The bleating of sheep, eager for fresh grass, greeted Ned
and Rebecca as they opened the pens. The horses worked
smoothly, urging the sheep ahead to where they would pasture that day.

Sunshine warmed the tops of Rebecca's bare hands as
the curtain of ruffled clouds parted to reveal a clear blue
sky. She remembered the relentless rays of the summer sun
and the freckles she'd acquired as a child.

Spending years in a dark house in Sydney and a few
days on a coach had not prepared her fair skin for ranch
life. In self-defense against sunburn and a thousand new

freckles, Rebecca had chosen a dress with high neckline and long sleeves. A bonnet protected her face.

They rode in comfortable silence while Rebecca scanned the familiar landscape. A mob of kangaroos nestled in the shade of a eucalyptus. A joey's small head bobbed above its mother's pouch.

She had missed the animals. She wondered what had become of the stallion she had once longed to tame. Many childhood hours had been spent daydreaming of flying across the meadows, clinging to his back.

She patted her gentle mount and knew it was time to put childhood dreams behind her. The days were long past when her father had swung her onto the saddle behind him and thrilled her with a gallop across the salt grass that left her gasping for breath.

Her chest filled with a deep ache at the memory of those rides. She could not look at this land without remembering how much her father had loved it. She loved it too. Nothing would ever take her away again.

They reached fresh pasture and dismounted, moving among the sheep to check for leg sores and foot rot. The docile animals accepted the inspection amiably, regarding Rebecca with large oval eyes.

She ran her hand along the wool, glad that her father had chosen good stock that grew soft, curly wool. Though they owned only three hundred head, the wool should fetch a good price when Ned took it to the market in Sydney.

As the sheep scattered, Rebecca and Ned mounted to ride the outskirts and keep watch for dingoes. Sheep were helpless creatures that could not be left without guards or barriers. Dingoes maimed and slaughtered far more sheep than they would eat in a single night, and she didn't have any sheep to spare.

She wondered about Cole's fence, an ambitious but practical project. It would be a relief not to have to drive the sheep back to shelter each night to keep them safe from wild dogs.

Rebecca sighed, wishing she could afford to join the enterprise. But Ned had been right. Along with tending the sheep, it was too big a project for just the two of them. A fence would have to wait. Perhaps, after shearing season, she could spare enough money to hire someone on.

Something moved on the horizon and Rebecca tensed, unwilling to lose any sheep to canine hunters. Yet a moment of study identified two riders. Her heart fluttered with expectation. She straightened her bonnet, wishing she'd taken more care with her appearance that morning. She brushed stray tendrils from her face and squinted, hoping to recognize Cole. As the riders approached, she could tell neither man had hair dark enough to be Cole.

Ned pulled his horse alongside her. Company on the lonesome flats was a prospect to be relished. She expected to see approval on his face at the prospect of visitors. The distrust that filled his sharp eyes spawned a knot of fear in the pit of her stomach. Her excitement faded as the riders closed the gap.

Ned spoke sharply. "Head back to the ranch. I'll see what they want."

"Who are they?"

He jerked his rifle toward the riders. "No time to explain. Head back."

Without an argument, Rebecca circled the grazing sheep and galloped toward the ranch house, leaving Ned to face danger alone. She would not have forsaken him if she had thought to bring her father's rifle. Yet, unarmed, she could be of little help.

Hooves pounded behind her, and she turned to see a stocky blond man bent low in heated pursuit. He cut her off abruptly, blocking her escape. She held on tightly, barely managing to remain in the saddle as her roan reared in alarm.

Anger overshadowed her fear. She calmed the frightened horse and snapped, "You nearly got me thrown."

The man's sinister smile revealed crooked yellow teeth. "I came to pay a neighborly visit. Can't think why you'd rush off like that. Maybe your father forgot to teach you good manners."

Taking an instant dislike to him, Rebecca replied sharply, "There's nothing wrong with my manners."

His bulky body rested low in the saddle, like an unsightly growth on the back of his handsome horse. Rebecca wished her glare could dismount him and wipe the smirk from his face.

Ned rode up, rifle held on the second rider, a small man with a gaunt face, meager beard, and greasy brown hair. Ned shifted his rifle to cover the heavy man. His thumb rested on the trigger with the tension of a dingo watching an adder.

Scowling, he asked, "Are ye okay, Rebecca?"

She nodded. "I'm okay."

The heavy man's bold eyes performed a coarse assessment of her figure. "Rebecca. That's a pretty name. And you're a pretty girl, too."

"Who are you?" she demanded.

"Andrew Finley, your neighbor. I hope we get to know each other real well."

Rebecca frowned. "I've heard a great deal about you, Mr. Finley."

"Call me Andrew." He stroked his chin. "I hope you haven't been listening to the wrong people. There are some who would like to destroy my good name."

Rebecca caught her breath and gained a measure of composure. "I haven't met anyone who speaks highly of you. I'm afraid we'll have to remain neighbors instead of friends."

Finley laughed without mirth. "You have been listening

to the wrong people." He turned to his companion. "I take care of my own, don't I, Jess?"

"Yep."

Jess had a sallow complexion and dark hollow eyes. Rebecca shivered, disliking his demeanor as much as Finley's.

"Never meant to give you a fright. Just wanted to ride over and see if you were getting settled. Ned's a nervous old bloke. No reason to get all excited," Finley said.

Judging by Ned's finger on his trigger, Rebecca decided he must have had a reason to get excited. Her patience was stretched as thin as her nerves and she wished desperately to end this encounter. Perhaps a cool manner would discourage Finley from any further contact.

She summoned her most formal tone. "It was thoughtful of you to stop by, but Ned and I are busy with the sheep. So if there's nothing else . . ."

Something in Finley's eyes caused her to break off and swallow hard. They were sharp eyes, pale green, almost yellow. They studied her with a boldness that made her feel as though he owned her.

"Too bad about your father. It must be hard work for the two of you. Pretty girl like you shouldn't have to work sheep." His tone dripped sympathy that didn't reach his eyes. Even with her lack of worldly experience, Rebecca understood what he wanted from her.

"I like working sheep. I could never be happy as a house pet," she retorted.

Finley laughed. "She's got spirit. I like that."

Jess laughed as though Rebecca had made an amusing joke.

Ned raised the rifle. "The boss asked ye to leave."

An answering challenge sparked in Finley's eyes. "I wouldn't want to disobey the boss, would I?"

He stared coldly at Ned before turning his attention to Rebecca. "I still think we could be friends. Allow me to come calling."

Rebecca shook her head. "We have nothing in common, Mr. Finley."

He raised his eyebrows in mock surprise. "Don't you think so? Well, perhaps I'll come anyway."

He turned away without waiting for a reply. Jess followed like a trained pup. Rebecca stared at their retreating backs with a sense of relief.

Ned lowered his rifle. "He'll have to kill me before he gets his dirty hands on this ranch."

She jumped at the vehemence in Ned's outburst. Remembering the speculation that Finley had ordered G.W. killed, she asked, "Do you think he'd kill us?"

Ned's expression looked darker than a storm. "He'd do anything to get what he wants. Ye remember that."

Though the sheep floated like cotton balls among the tender grass and the sun still bathed them in its warmth, Rebecca's enjoyment of the scene was ruined. She tended her flock with a nervous eye toward the northern property line, where Finley and Jess had disappeared.

When it was time to drive the sheep home, tension had left her exhausted. The day had been longer than she expected, and altered her plan to come back soon enough to cook a decent supper. Cold lamb and bread would have to do. At least the cleanup would be easy.

After supper she sat on the porch with Ned. The sun rested like a bright orange ball on the edge of the horizon. Wisps of clouds clung in the pale blue sky, waiting for the camouflage of night. Shadows lengthened under the trees and the grasshoppers began their nightly chants.

A mild breeze ruffled the hem of her dress. Though it did little to cool her, the movement of air provided relief from the stuffy house that had collected heat during the afternoon. Memories of childhood forged a bittersweet path to her heart. Sunset had been Rebecca's favorite time of day. After her mother retired early, complaining of a headache or other ailment, her father had sat on the porch with

Ned until bright stars appeared in the black velvet sky. Rebecca curled in his lap, listening to them talk until sleep overtook her.

A pang of loneliness brought tears to her eyes. She wiped them away and determined not to give in to fatigue or fear. She and Ned would run this sheep station by the sweat of their brows. It would grow and prosper and make her father proud.

She glanced at Ned, his knife busy with a block of wood he kept on the porch for whittling. Rebecca watched, feeling soothed by the comfortable memory of other nights, nights long ago, when she'd watched him work.

"You carved a set of animals for me when I was a little girl. Do you remember?"

Ned nodded. "I remember." He continued his project without looking up.

"You gave me a kangaroo, a koala, a sheep, a dingo, and a horse. I pretended the horse was the wild stallion I longed to tame. I sat on the porch and made the horse chase the dingo away from the sheep."

Ned grinned. "Ye've always had a good imagination. Ye wore our ears off talking for hours about how ye were going to tame that horse."

"I finally gave up," she said softly. She remembered the disappointment she'd felt when she'd accepted the fact that she could never tame the stallion. He would never love her or be her pet. A tiny part of her heart died with the acceptance that dreams did not always come true.

It was part of growing up, she'd told herself. Love was a two-way road. Even if she loved something did not mean it loved her in return. To avoid further disappointment, she had set about to rid herself of her silly romantic notions. Yet, hard as she had tried, she knew a portion of the dreamer refused to give way.

"I still have those wooden animals," she admitted. "I brought them to Sydney and back. The whole while I lived with Aunt Abigail I was afraid she would find them and say I was too old for toys and make me give them away. So I kept them under my bed. They were all I had, except memories, to remind me of my life here. I felt I would die if I lost them, too."

Ned snorted. "Ye never belonged in Sydney. I told Roger he ought to go and fetch ye back, but he couldn't be sure it was right to be taking ye from yer mother."

Rebecca stared at the horizon where the sun had gone from orange to pink. "I was miserable there. I kept reminding myself of how I was taught that everything would work out for good. It was so hard to believe. But now I'm back and no one can take me away."

The past was behind her. But she had the future. She hoped, someday, to have children of her own to sit on this porch and play with the wooden animals as she had done. She imagined a little boy who had dark eyes like Cole's.

She frowned at her wayward imagination. She felt like a little girl again, reaching for the untamable stallion. This time she would stop herself before her imagination allowed her to get hurt.

Chapter six

Cole wiped his damp forehead and squinted into the sky. The blistering sun was finally melting from hot yellow to a mellow pink on the horizon, signaling the end of a long day. He had spent all morning with the sheep and all afternoon working on the fence. Only one more post to sink, and then a Saturday evening to stretch his legs on the porch and relax.

He'd drink a cup of ale and play a few hands of cards with his mates. Maybe G.W. would join them if he felt up to it. After the stress of the last week, they could all use some time to unwind.

With annoyance, he realized that he wondered what Rebecca would think of his plans. He never drank to excess and rarely lost money on cards. Still, he had the uncomfortable feeling she would disapprove. The thought bothered him.

Cole lowered the end of the post into the dirt and packed the earth into place with his boot. Then he pounded the nail that attached the post to the expanding wall. Distracted by his thoughts of Rebecca, he let the hammer graze the side of his thumb. He squeezed his sore thumb against his leg and growled in pain.

It served him right for taking his mind off his business. It wasn't like he didn't have plenty here to keep him busy without letting his thoughts wander to things that didn't concern him. He stoically reminded himself that life was unpredictable and hard. His mother's death had convinced him it was painful to care deeply about any human being. The pain of loss cut too deeply. Better to embrace loneliness.

The throbbing eased, but his swollen thumb reminded him that despite his resolve, Rebecca's opinion meant more to him than he cared to admit. Hadn't his determination to avoid her crumbled yesterday when he'd looked into her eyes? He could still hear the lilt of her voice when she thanked him for his help. He shook his head, wishing he could shake away his thoughts.

After securing the post securely to the growing length of fence, Cole headed back to the ranch with his crew. He washed at the pump before following the aroma of Davies's cooking. On Saturday nights, Cole ate in the dining room with G.W.

He stepped into the house and stopped short at the sight of his boss. Though his arm still hung in a sling, G.W. was dressed in a shirt that was clean and pressed. His sandy hair was parted and combed. Cole frowned as he watched G.W. put the finishing shine on his best boots.

"Going somewhere?" he asked.

G.W. glanced up. A blush of red brightened his already ruddy features. "Rebecca invited me to supper. She told me to bring along a book. I thought poetry might be a good choice." He shrugged with a helpless grin.

Cole's dark brows creased into a deeper frown. "It's too soon for you to be riding. And that arm puts you at a disadvantage if you were to meet trouble."

"If you're so worried, you could come with me." Amusement shone in G.W.'s amber eyes, deepening at Cole's dilemma. Cole knew there'd be no stopping him. Yet, he did not relish spending an evening listening to poems.

He grimaced in irritation as G.W. waited placidly for his reply, although the rancher already knew the outcome. Cole sighed in surrender. "I'll get cleaned up and come with you."

G.W. grinned. "Better hurry."

The blood-red sun dipped onto the horizon as they headed to Rebecca's ranch. Cole's edgy fingers lay close to his thigh so he could reach his gun on a second's notice.

He squinted, scouring the shadows under each tree, looking for figures hiding beneath the deepening cover of dusk. A kangaroo emerged from his shady retreat, and Cole whipped out his gun at the movement.

Feeling foolish, Cole glanced over to see if G.W. had noticed his mistake. But his boss chattered on, oblivious to Cole's unease as he continued a running account of his plans to win Rebecca's affection. He didn't pause until they came in sight of her house.

G.W. pulled up abruptly and straightened in his saddle. "Do I look okay?" he asked Cole.

Despite his desire not to be there, Cole had to smile. G.W. reminded him of a small boy who hoped to please his teacher.

Cole pretended to survey him intensely. "You look great, except for that simple-minded grin. Looks like you're hoping she won't throw you out if you forgot to wash behind your ears."

G.W.'s smile faded to a look of chagrin. "She's too kind for that. But ladies being few and far between out here, I don't want to do anything to offend her."

Cole nodded, feeling ashamed of treating G.W.'s earnest desire to impress Rebecca so lightly. He shifted in the saddle and relaxed from his rigid position.

He gave G.W. a serious appraisal. "Any girl would be

proud to have you come calling. Before long, she'll be begging to be your wife."

Saying the words caused a strange hollowness to form in Cole's heart. He wondered if his earlier desire to needle G.W. had sprung from envy. But envy didn't change the truth.

G.W.'s cherubic face lit with embarrassed pleasure. "I don't guess she'll be begging. I just hope, someday, she's willing to have me."

They dismounted in the yard near the chicken coop, and G.W. patted down his slick hair. He grinned as Ned looked up from the porch and called an enthusiastic greeting.

Doubting the enthusiasm included him, Cole reached for G.W.'s reins. "I'll tie the horses while you go inside."

G.W. strode forward, eager to greet Ned and more eager to see Rebecca. She had not appeared on the porch; Cole assumed she was inside sprucing up for G.W.

Not that there was much she needed to do to enhance her looks. Cole remembered the silky pale hair that framed her face. Her creamy skin contrasted with her dark lashes, drawing attention to eyes of the clearest azure blue.

If looks weren't enough, she had an independent spirit that would keep any man on his toes. Most women would have sold the ranch and headed back as soon as they found themselves sole owner of a sheep station.

He knew Rebecca would have come even if she'd known in advance about her father's death. She had a self-sufficient and untamed quality that excited and challenged Cole. She loved the outback as much as any man he'd ever met. G.W. was a lucky man to be courting her, for she was like no other woman Cole had ever known.

He tied the horses and glanced at the deserted porch. A light burned in the kitchen. By the looks of things everyone had gone in without him.

He struggled with relief and disappointment. He warned himself that Rebecca surely knew the truth by now and just as surely hated him. It was best to avoid her by sitting on the porch until G.W. came out.

His resolve faltered as she stepped into the doorway, looking like an angel, backlit by the soft glow of lantern light.

"I thought you might like some supper. And I have fresh cake and coffee."

Rebecca wore a simple cotton dress that followed the shape of her slender figure. Her silky hair was captured in a loose bun at the nape of her neck, but rebellious tendrils escaped on each side.

Her shaky smile seemed tentative and unsure. Cole guessed, from her expression, that Ned hadn't yet told her about his part in her father's death.

He let out a tight breath of relief. Though he did not understand why he'd been spared, he felt like a prisoner given a last reprieve.

She would find out someday. It was inevitable. And then she would despise him. But tonight, he could not resist the warmth of her smile or the invitation in her eyes. Like a moth drawn to a candle, he would enjoy the light before the flame could burn him.

The aroma of freshly baked dessert rewarded Cole's decision to put aside his better judgment and follow her into the house. The kitchen presented a scene of domestic warmth. The lamp encircled the table and the occupants of the chairs in a friendly, welcoming light. A dented coffeepot and bowls of stew sat on the table, and a sugar-glazed cake sat in the center.

Ned and G.W. glanced up from their stew. G.W. grinned. "You better dig in before it's gone. Don't tell Davies, but I'd trade him any day for a cook like this."

Rebecca's cheeks flushed to a soft rose.

Cole ate his stew and then accepted a slice of cake, savoring the warmth of Rebecca's hand as their fingers met in the exchange. She glanced down, swiftly hiding her eyes beneath her dark lashes and capturing her bottom lip between her teeth. Was she aware of the effect these small gestures had on him? Cole wondered.

Ned and G.W. discussed shearing schedules while Cole and Rebecca ate in silence. Cole felt sure his attraction to her had to be written all over his face.

He sipped his coffee and watched her eyes flit between the speakers, and would have given a great deal to know what she was thinking.

Rebecca sensed Cole's gaze and deliberately avoided it. Her hand still tingled from his touch, and she didn't trust her eyes to hide the confusion it had evoked. The intensely masculine strength of his presence tugged at her, forcing her to pretend immunity when every nerve was coiled into taut awareness.

At last the men were sated. They set down their forks and pushed back in their chairs. Ned excused himself for a smoke on the porch while Rebecca accepted the poetry book and scanned the contents.

They waited expectantly until she began to read a poem comparing the cycles of nature to the journeys of life. In the sweet torture of her endless words, Cole wondered if G.W., like himself, was less affected by her words than the sound of her voice.

When the poem ended at last, stars winked at the pale moon as Cole and G.W. plodded on their horses back to the ranch. In the distance, a lyrebird uttered a lonely cry.

Cole glanced at the dark silhouette of his boss's face as G.W. said, "I've never thought much about the deeper meaning of life. Been too busy living, I guess. How about you?"

In the years he'd lived under Andrew Finley's roof, Cole had found that stifling his opinions made life less painful. Self-preservation had conditioned him to keep his mouth shut. Now that there was no penalty, the bitterness he had accumulated spilled out. "I never found much sense in how a frail woman and a boy could end up at the mercy of Andrew Finley."

G.W. rode in silence. The night air carried the fragrance of wild orchids. Cole breathed deeply, trying to cleanse his body of the haunting memories. If G.W. wanted to chase after the meaning of life, that was his business. Cole had no such interest.

He had almost put the conversation from his mind when G.W. said, "Maybe it's not good for us when everything's real easy. Hard times make tough people."

Cole didn't reply.

G.W. continued, talking as much to himself as to Cole, "Take Rebecca, for example. She has every right to be bitter, coming out here as she did and finding her father dead. But it only seems to have made her stronger, more determined."

Cole's head began to ache. Perhaps there was something to live for besides the anger and bitterness that had sustained him. It had been a long time since he'd examined his childhood feelings. Perhaps he'd been missing something. Yet he sensed he would have to give up the anger and bitterness in order to embrace the unknown. He massaged the dull ache that had settled in his forehead. He tried to ignore the questions that rose to the surface of his mind, demanding answers. Most likely, he was just tired. Tomorrow he would forget this foolishness and be back in control.

The ranch loomed ahead, familiar and inviting. Cole urged his horse forward, yearning to reach the bunkhouse, where he could lose his uncertainty in the oblivion of sleep.

On Sunday morning, Rebecca found it impossible to forget the emotions that had crossed Cole's face. She ached for him to find a release from his painful past. It would take time, she reminded herself. She would have to be patient.

Leaving Ned to tend the sheep, she rode back to the

shack at noon to prepare their lunch. Perhaps the change
of scenery would help her restless mind focus. It took patience to devote long hours to guarding the flock. Today,
the monotony had given Rebecca too much time to think.

The house greeted her with its customary stuffy smell of
old furniture and dusty rugs. A sunbeam fell across the
table, illuminating floating flecks of dust suspended in the
midair. She wrinkled her nose, remembering the mouse
Ned caught scurrying under the sofa. She would give the
house a good cleaning when she found the time. For now,
tending to the daily needs of the animals and cooking the
meals took all of her time.

She brushed her damp hair from her forehead. The un-
remitting sun warmed the little kitchen. In spite of the heat,
she was determined to show Ned how much she appreci-
ated his loyalty and friendship. She lit the stove and began
to prepare a chicken for frying. As it cooked, she collected
biscuits and a can of beans for a picnic lunch she'd carry
back to share with Ned.

Rebecca sang while she worked. Her singing, along with
the rustling and clattering of her cooking, kept her from
hearing the whinny of a horse as a rider slipped into the
ranch yard. The creak of the door alerted her that she had
company. She stopped singing and frowned. Ned would
never leave the sheep unattended. In a few minutes, dingoes
could slaughter half a dozen or more. And who besides Ned
would walk into the house without calling out a greeting?

She spun around to see Andrew Finley's bulky frame
blocking her doorway. An involuntary gasp escaped as she
realized she was alone and trapped. The threat she had felt
when she faced him on the open grassland was nothing
compared to the fear seizing her now, cornered in her own
home.

For a moment, Finley stared at her, his only movement
in his slack jowl, working a wad of tobacco. His pale eyes
seemed to calculate her reaction to his sudden arrival.

He spat on the floor and Rebecca jumped. In spite of her determination to hold her ground, she took a step back. She knew by the look on his face that her retreat was a mistake. He gave a perverse smile at her response.

"That was pretty singing. I'd like to put you in a cage and have you all to myself so you could sing for me." The hunger in his eyes betrayed the selfishness behind the compliment.

Rebecca narrowed her eyes. "I didn't invite you into my house." She forced herself to calm her breathing. "I'm expecting Ned any time for lunch. Why don't you state your business and be out of here?"

Finley shook his heavy head. His unkempt brows drew up in feigned surprise. "Ned's tending the sheep. I don't think he's coming home. I think he's waiting for you to bring lunch. But he won't mind if you're a little late."

He stepped forward and Rebecca reached for the rolling pin. She felt a wave of nausea rise in her throat. Her heart pounded so hard she felt it would surely break through her ribs. She knew that if he touched her she was sure to be sick.

He paused, regarding her in mock surprise. "Why so jumpy? I only intended to see what you were cooking. It smells good. I could use a good cook. Maybe you'd let me share your lunch."

Rebecca scowled. "I'm not finished cooking it."

Finley strolled to the table and plucked a biscuit from the half-dozen that sat nestled in a checked napkin. Rebecca retreated deeper into the corner.

He placed his boot on the seat of a chair and regarded her, careful to stay out of range of her weapon. "Go on with your work. It would be a shame to burn that crispy chicken."

She shook her head. "I'll finish when you leave."

He took his time chewing the biscuit, making a show of savoring the last bite. Wiping his sleeve across his mouth, he regarded her coldly. "There's no reason to be so unfriendly. I only came to talk. I want to offer you a business arrangement, as a favor to you."

She frowned, sensing his game of intimidation was only beginning. Still, if she heard him out, perhaps he would agree to go.

Attempting to take charge of the situation, Rebecca said, "Sit down and don't move while I turn the chicken. I'll listen, but I doubt I'll be interested in anything you have to offer."

Finley took a chair across the table and eyed her with the interest of a spider waiting for a fly to land in his web. He folded his beefy hands and said, "You're a good-looking woman and I admire your spirit. I'd like to help you out. You and the old man can't keep this shack standing forever. You marry me and I'll let the old man stay on here. My boys can run both the ranches and you'll live better than you ever could here."

Still clutching the rolling pin, Rebecca turned back to face him. Despite her fear, she nearly laughed at the smug expression on his face. "You expect me to believe you want to marry me to make my life more comfortable? Could it really be that you want to get your sheep to easier water?"

Finley's eyes narrowed to slits. The change came so swiftly that Rebecca drew a shuddered breath and sidled toward the doorway. He was on his feet in an instant, cutting off her escape. "I don't have to ask you to marry me, you know."

She heard his breathing, rapid and shallow, like a predator excited by the challenge of a chase. Her knees trembled so violently that she wondered if they would carry her if she got the chance to escape.

"I'll marry G.W. before I let you get your hands on this ranch," she whispered.

Finley charged forward so swiftly that Rebecca barely had time to swing the rolling pin. She landed a sharp blow into his hand before he wrenched the weapon from her grasp. His powerful fingers gripped her arm so tightly she cried out in pain.

His face came close to hers, his pale eyes inches from her own. "I'll have to see that G.W. doesn't stay healthy enough to marry you. These are dangerous times. Perhaps he'll meet with an accident."

"No!" Rebecca gasped. Fear for G.W. filled her heart.

"Then you'd better be smart and come with me. We'll go to town and get married. You'll deed me your ranch and I'll have no hard feelings toward G.W."

She stared into the cold eyes and felt her blood chill. "I would never marry you." She jerked violently, hoping to pull free. But his grip only tightened until all she could feel was pain.

"Like it or not, I'll have you and your ranch," he sneered as he pulled her from the kitchen.

The memory of Cole's powerful shoulders, his strong hands, filled her mind. She needed him. She wished he would come before it was too late. She screamed and scratched at her captor, desperate for rescue, yet knowing Cole was too far away to hear her.

Chapter seven

Finley propelled Rebecca onto the porch. She gave a whimper of relief when they ran headlong into Ned's shotgun, aimed at Finley's chest. "Let her go," Ned growled. The cold fury in his tone left no room for argument.

Finley hesitated a moment, staring into Ned's determined face, before he loosened his hold. Rebecca jerked away and flew to Ned's side.

"He hurt you?" Ned asked, without taking his eyes off Finley.

Rebecca rubbed her arm. She took a deep breath to calm herself. "No. Not really."

Finley scowled. "We were talking business."

Ned's eyes narrowed. "Didn't look to me like Rebecca liked the terms. Get out of here before my finger gets too heavy."

Finley stalked past them, turning to glare at Ned as he swung onto his horse. "You'll be sorry for this, old man."

Rebecca shivered. Feeling lightheaded, she grasped Ned's arm and allowed him to steer her into the house. She accepted a cup of cool water and sank into a chair to sip it while Ned lifted the browned chicken from the pan.

"How did you know he was here? You were too far away to hear me," she said as she regained her composure.

"I saw a speck of a rider heading fast for the house. I knew we weren't expecting company."

"I'm glad you have good eyesight." She smiled fondly, loving every line in his wrinkled face.

Feeling better now, Rebecca began to help bundle up the food. She hated to think what might become of the sheep while Ned was away.

"You're going to stay with me from now on, and carry a gun, too," Ned asserted.

Rebecca paused long enough to clean the floor where Finley had spat, desiring to expunge any evidence of his presence. She put the rag aside to be burned and followed Ned to the horses. The warm breeze on her face and the sun on the back of her thin cotton dress comforted her. She drew a deep breath. The air had never felt as sweet.

They reached the flock and began to round up stragglers. Scouting the grasses, they were relieved to find that no dingoes had found the unprotected sheep.

When they had accounted for the whole flock, they spread their dinner in the shade of a large gum tree. Rebecca attempted to eat, but found she had little appetite. She couldn't forget the look in Finley's eyes when he'd threatened to murder G.W. The experience she'd had that afternoon left no doubt that he was capable of such an act.

And what would stop him? She could never convince G.W. to hide. The attack he had already suffered had not dissuaded him from coming to court her. She doubted she could convince him to stay home.

Rebecca was too absorbed in her thoughts to notice Ned's troubled eyes. She looked up with a start when he said, "You're worried about Finley, as you should be. We're going to have to be extra careful from now on."

She nodded. "He scares me out of my wits. But not just

for my sake. He threatened to kill G.W. so I couldn't marry him. He'll do it, too. He's already tried."

Ned rubbed his grizzled chin. "I'm not sure there's much you can do."

Rebecca stood and brushed down her skirt with a decisive gesture. "I don't think G.W. will listen to me, but I can think of someone he might listen to. I'm going to ride over and see if Cole's working on the fence."

Ned frowned. His bushy brows drew together. "I don't know if that's going to do any good. Could be Cole already knows Finley's plans for G.W."

She frowned. "So do I. But I'm hoping Cole can talk G.W. into laying low for awhile."

Ned sighed. "You're not going alone. We'll take the sheep in early and I'll ride out with you."

When the three hundred white bobbing heads had been safely penned, Ned and Rebecca rode to the eastern edge of G.W.'s property. In the distance, Rebecca spotted the small crew hammering together each board of the fence. She recognized Cole's tall frame long before he saw her coming, and pushed aside the guilty knowledge that she would have liked to stay where she was and watch him work, to see the strong muscles in his back ripple when he lifted a board, his long slender fingers holding each new section in place. She did not pause for even a hoofbeat to entertain her errant wish, but she could not deny its existence.

Rebecca saw Cole's reaction when his sharp senses alerted him to their approach. He reached for his rifle, then set it quickly against the fence as he identified her and Ned.

Rebecca's heartbeat quickened despite her attempt to ignore the effect Cole's gaze had on her. She fancied a spark of pleasure in his dark eyes and chastised herself for an active imagination.

Cole strode forward, shadowed by a quickly grinning Wally. Rebecca swallowed hard and averted her eyes from the fine coils of dark hair that escaped the front of Cole's half-buttoned shirt.

"I was hoping to catch you here. I have something important to discuss." She felt suddenly timid.

Cole studied her carefully. Seeming to sense her concern, he said, "Let's sit under the tree where it's cooler."

The men continued their work as Cole led the way to a shady gum tree. The leafy branches protected them from the sun, but not from the heat that seemed to exude from the ground.

Rebecca fingered her skirt nervously as she plunged into the reason for her visit. "Andrew Finley barged in while I was cooking dinner. He insisted that I marry him, and then threatened to kill G.W. after I turned him down." She paused to catch her breath and realized the experience had unnerved her more than she had been willing to admit.

She saw Cole stiffen. Looking into his eyes, she explained, "He thinks he can force me to marry him by taking away my other choices. G.W. won't listen to me, but maybe he'll listen to you. He has to stay away from me, to stay close to home. I couldn't bear to live with my conscience if anything bad happened to him."

"She hasn't told you everything," Ned broke in. "I came home in time to find your stepfather hauling her onto the porch to carry her off."

Cole's eyes bore into Ned with thinly controlled rage. "I claim no kin with him. He never hesitated to trample on me when I got in his way."

He turned to Rebecca and his voice became softer. "Did he hurt you?"

She shook her head, surprised by the tears that welled in her eyes. "Will you talk to G.W.?"

Cole shook his head. "You don't turn tail and run from

a man like Finley. He'll hunt you down and kill you like a sick wallaby," he explained slowly.

He looked deep into her eyes and continued, "The only thing Finley respects is strength. G.W. would tell you the same thing. He won't let Finley keep him away. That's what he wants. Still, I'll talk G.W. into sending Wally and a few of the men out on patrol when we come on Saturday. We'll be ready if Finley's men are lying in wait."

Rebecca's fears subsided with the assurance in Cole's eyes. Cole knew Finley. He knew how to handle him. And his devotion to G.W. was obvious. He would see to his protection.

"Be careful," she whispered.

Cole met her shy gaze with frank concern. "You're the one who needs to be careful. Finley's as ruthless as they come when he's prevented from getting what he wants."

"I'm not letting her out of my sight, or the sight of this," Ned said, raising his rifle.

"We'll be careful," Rebecca promised. She still could not take her eyes off Cole's face. "We better get back."

Cole nodded. "I'll see you safely to the house."

Ned shook his head. "No need," he said. His brusque tone nettled Rebecca.

"If you're busy, it's not necessary," she said, hoping to smooth over Ned's rudeness.

"I'd feel better. I'm going to tell Wally to keep an eye on your place at night. If anything moves, he'll see it."

Rebecca frowned slightly. "I can't repay your consideration."

"Yes you can. You can stay out of Finley's clutches. That would be payment enough for me." Cole's voice betrayed his bitterness.

He rode with them to the edge of the ranch yard. Rebecca waved and watched him ride away when she reached the barn. She followed Ned as he busied himself putting the horses up for the night. She decided to bring up what was on her mind.

"You don't like Cole, do you?"

Ned didn't look up from brushing his horse. "I don't trust him."

"But I don't see why you have any reason not to trust him. He truly hates Finley."

"Or pretends to." He set the brush on the tack shelf and turned to Rebecca. "There's something I haven't told you, because I don't have any way to prove that it was intentional."

Rebecca bit her lip. Something about Ned's hesitation made her wish she hadn't broached the subject. She was tempted to tell him she'd changed her mind; if it was anything bad about Cole she didn't want to know. Still, she knew curiosity would get the best of her.

"Your father had left the wagon with Cole to have the wheel rebuilt. He was on the way home when the accident happened," Ned said flatly.

"So . . . I don't see," Rebecca began, and then paused suddenly, her eyes growing wide. "You're saying Cole fixed the wagon so it would break?"

Ned looked away. "He knew you were coming. If he was working with Finley, it was the perfect time to put you on your own. You'd be forced to marry Finley or else sell him the ranch and scurry back to Sydney. Only thing was, they didn't figure on G.W."

Rebecca's stomach churned in revulsion at the idea that Cole could be responsible for her father's death. "It can't be. Cole hates Andrew Finley. He's said as much." Yet in the face of Ned's suspicion, her objection sounded weak.

Rebecca ate a light dinner and retired to her room to stare gloomily out the window, feeling her spirits sink with the rosy glow of the setting sun. She shivered as darkness fell, not from cold, but from the knowledge that when she woke up in the morning, things would not be the same.

A cloud of suspicion hung in her mind, threatening the fantasy she had nurtured like a fragile orchid. She had felt a growing kinship with Cole. They had both survived childhoods in which they had been forced to struggle for self-respect. She had thought that, like her, he had left home in order to keep his past from poisoning his future.

He could still be innocent. But why would the wheel have come off so soon after being fixed? Finley had said he took care of his own. Could it be that he'd offered Cole an inheritance to help get his hands on this property? The timing was perfect. With Rebecca being the only heir, Finley could rid himself of her father and gain a wife and a sheep ranch.

She thought about Cole's intense dark eyes, the tremor of barely controlled rage in his voice when he spoke of Finley. She found it impossible to imagine seeds of treachery taking root. But could she be sure? She barely knew Cole.

Weariness drained her of the energy to puzzle it out. She slid into bed and closed her eyes, trying to ignore the aching bruises on her arms left from her struggle with Finley.

Cole had promised to post Wally as a lookout. Yet Wally had made it clear that his loyalty lay with Cole. Could either of them be trusted?

Her mind drifted to the words Wally had spoken on G.W.'s porch. Wally had assured her that Cole was taken with her. If that was true, it made no sense that he would help Finley in any way. But nothing made sense anymore.

Rebecca awoke on Saturday morning wondering if Cole would accompany G.W. to see her. She was uncertain how she felt about facing him. The week had seemed to drag along. Restless nights and watchful days had left her raw-nerved and dispirited. Even knowing that Ned slept in the lean-to with a gun at hand did not serve to lessen the jitters that beset her each night.

A kookaburra began its shrill call, ending in a cackling laugh. Rebecca shuddered. If Cole were in a plot with Finley, there was no doubt he was laughing at the foolish girl who had shown such naïve gratitude toward him. The thought made her angry and depressed.

Rebecca determined to put Cole out of her mind. Confronting him with the circumstances of her father's death would do no good. She could not be sure she could trust his explanation. She only hoped that he would prove his innocence beyond a doubt. Until then, she would treat Cole McBride with suspicion.

As promised, Cole sent a small party of men to inspect the route before he accompanied G.W. to Rebecca's ranch. He felt a deep weight of responsibility, not only because of his fondness for G.W., but because he did not want to fail Rebecca's trust. To that purpose, he was prepared to die if need be.

After the men came back, reporting that the trail was clear, Cole sent them to the bunkhouse to play cards. Then he collected G.W., who had scrubbed his already florid face to a rosy glow and had slicked back his thin sandy hair.

Even though the men had swept their trail, Cole kept alert. His eyes roved the grasses but found nothing but kangaroos grazing peacefully on a gentle upsweep and parrots flashing riotous colors as they dashed from tree to tree. Only when they reached Rebecca's porch did Cole become aware of the lingering warmth of the evening and the scent of wildflowers blooming beside the house.

G.W. cleared his throat nervously and wiped perspiration from his brow. He looked like a wax doll melting in the heat. Cole smiled in spite of his agitation.

He thought about his conversation with Wally on the day that Ned and Rebecca had ridden out to see him. Wally had insisted Rebecca favored Cole as a suitor. It was silly talk. Cole had chided himself for paying it any attention. He had nothing to offer her, yet, he could not seem to quell the small flame of possibility that Wally had ignited.

The aroma of rhubarb pie and strong coffee beckoned them into the kitchen. Cole's heart beat a little faster when he saw Rebecca. She stood with her back to him, facing the stove. He allowed himself a moment to savor her slender figure and soft hair falling in a cascade about her shoulders. The apron tied above the womanly curve of her hips accentuated her tiny waist.

Cole might have thought his feelings sprang only from the appreciation of her beauty if not for the pleasure he took in being with her, looking into her eyes, and listening to her speak. His interest in Rebecca went far beyond physical attraction. He felt a soul-stirring kinship that he could not control, a desire to share his deepest thoughts and needs with another human being. The vulnerability frightened him, yet pulled him like a bee to nectar.

She turned and their eyes met. In that brief moment, he saw the pain of betrayal. She looked away without smiling, her smooth forehead wrinkled into a frown. Cole's heart sank as he watched her focus more attention than necessary into slicing the pie.

As the evening wore on, Rebecca's attitude towards him remained decidedly cool. Cole knew there could be only one explanation. She'd been told he'd fixed the wagon that her father drove to his death. Ned had probably told her that, when Cole repaired a hub, it didn't break accidentally.

And Ned would be right. That was why Roger had asked him to fix the wagon. Nobody did better repairs than Cole. So what could he say if she asked him? He didn't understand it, either. He'd fixed that wheel with as much care as any other.

Cole found it impossible to concentrate on her reading. When G.W. became absorbed in a particularly deep passage of poetry, Cole slipped from the kitchen. He was tired of feeling Ned's distrust boring into his back, sharp as a knife's blade.

He knew Ned believed him to be cut from the same cloth as Finley. A traitor. Ned would spend the rest of the evening with one hand on his shotgun, expecting Cole to summon his stepfather's men for a charge on the house.

Cole stepped off the porch, uncertain of where to go. His fists clenched tightly against his muscular thighs were the only sign of the frustration at life that he had learned to suppress. Through he felt drowned in a sea of misery, his senses were alert. A movement beside the corral brought a lightning-fast draw of his gun. If Finley's men were out there, he would go down fighting. At least then no one could accuse him of having invited them.

A lone figure stepped from the shadows. Cole recognized Wally. "I could have shot you," he growled as Wally approached.

Wally reacted with a smile. The moonlight lit his broad face, and his eyes reflected confidence in Cole. "You'd never shoot without knowing who was there."

Cole nodded as he replaced his gun. His aim, though deadly accurate, was always sure of its target.

Wally frowned. "Why aren't you inside with the missy?"

Cole felt as though a hot knife had turned in his heart. He grimaced. "There's no hope. She thinks I killed her father and I have no way to prove otherwise. She'll marry G.W. and spend the rest of her life hating me."

Wally shook his head. "Not that one. She follows her heart. That's why she's here." He spread his arms to encompass the ranch.

Cole didn't feel like arguing. Still, he had known when he looked into Rebecca's eyes that nothing short of a miracle would erase the accusation he'd seen.

He took a short walkabout with Wally, finding solace in the aborigine's silent company. Although he didn't agree with Wally's simple faith in life's happy endings, he did believe a loyal friend could ease the pain.

When G.W. appeared on the porch, Wally left to begin his night watch in the deep shadows of the house. Cole readied the horses, then waited impatiently until G.W. said his goodbyes and joined him.

They rode along in silence until G.W. said, "I never understood poetry before. Never really tried, I guess," he added with a chuckle. Sobering he said, "Now, it's making a lot of sense."

Cole noticed the excitement in his voice. Surely Rebecca had also noticed G.W.'s enthusiasm. No doubt she approved. Enough to marry him?

"You've never had such a pretty teacher before," he suggested, trying to keep his tone light.

"No, that's not it," G.W. insisted. His voice held an earnest timbre. "It would make sense now even if it was an old grizzled schoolmaster who helped me learn. And the more I read, the more I enjoy it."

When Cole didn't reply, G.W. gave him a measured look.

Cole merely clenched his jaw. He found it unlikely that he would be included in any more lessons.

Chapter eight

On Monday morning, Rebecca saw Wally appear from his all-night vigil behind the gum tree. While he stretched, she wrapped freshly baked biscuits in a clean dishcloth and hurried to offer them to him. Wally accepted the warm bread with the wide grin that he always wore.

She lingered outside, watching as he carried the food away as though it was a prize. She savored the last scent of the cool morning breeze. Soon, the blistering sun would turn the dewy ground into a sauna. Already, the high puffy clouds were fleeing and the sky held no promise of rain.

Her hair felt damp against her forehead when she returned to the kitchen. She brushed it back and swept crumbs from the plank floor that felt pleasantly cool under her bare feet.

Ned finished his coffee and rinsed his cup. "I'll get the horses."

Rebecca knew she'd been dawdling and would have to hurry to pack a lunch. She smiled to herself as she mentally ticked off the chores for the day. Wally's night watch had allowed her to sleep without waking up a dozen times to worry about an unfamiliar sound. She felt good today, good enough to tackle a hot day of watching the grazing sheep.

Ned got his hat. She heard his boots thump across the front porch. She set the broom in the corner and decided to ask whether he'd like chicken or mutton for his noon meal. She hustled toward the living room to catch him before he left to get the horses.

She heard him groan and wondered if a wild creature had entered the chicken yard during the night to kill her hens and leave a mess of feathers. Ned had a right to groan. It wouldn't be a pretty sight.

The thud of a body changed the direction of her thoughts. Rebecca's heart pounded as she dashed to the door. Ned lay motionless on his face, sprawled across the last porch step. Before she could kneel beside him, hard fingers closed around her arm.

She gasped as she stared into the cold gray eyes of Jess, the man who had accompanied Finley on his last visit. Rebecca wrenched violently, breaking Jess's grip. Yet, before she could run, two men climbed the steps to join them. The bigger man grabbed Rebecca's shoulders and thrust her hard against the house.

The back of her head ached as it hit the hard wood. Her lungs felt tight with panic as heavy palms pinned her shoulders against the wall.

"It's been a long time since I've seen anything half as pretty as you," he growled, his breath holding the stale stench of whiskey. She pushed at his arms and tried to break away.

He pressed closer. "What's your hurry?" His pitted face loomed toward hers.

Rebecca turned her face to avoid him and felt his hard fingers dig into her shoulders. Before he could make another attempt, Jess said, "Boss says not to touch her, Lem. Unless you want to waltz matilda, we better take her back."

The big man apparently decided that Finley was serious in his threat to hang anyone who touched Rebecca. He dragged her toward the large roan and said, "You're riding with me."

Her shock gave way to panic. She had no intention of becoming the property of Andrew Finley. The idea of living in his house sickened her.

With every muscle in her body, she resolved not to let them put her on the horse. She fought and scratched and managed to land a hard kick on Lem's shin. He cursed in rage as the other two men wrestled her onto the saddle.

The horse whinnied as Rebecca's captor climbed on. He held her with a vise-like grip so tight she could hardly breathe. His chest pressed against her back, and she could feel the rise and fall of his exerted breathing through the thin fabric of her cotton dress.

She shuddered and gave way to the sobs that choked her throat. Hadn't Finley told her he was used to getting what he wanted? He wanted her and, in the captivity of these three men, she realized there was little hope for escape.

The big man kicked the roan into a gallop. The scenery sped by in a nauseating blur. Terror rose in Rebecca's chest, and instinct told her to scream, to fight and resist. But Lem's strong arm compressed her lungs so much she could barely cling to consciousness.

How long would it be before anyone noticed what had happened? They had abducted her before she could learn how badly Ned was injured. If he was still alive, he might lie there for days, badly hurt and needing help. And help might not come until Wally came to keep watch that night.

By then she would have spent all day with Finley. She shuddered and closed her eyes, her stomach lurching in revulsion. Would anyone dare face his well-fortified ranch to come for her?

G.W. would surely want to help. But would any of his hands join him? Tears squeezed from Rebecca's eyes as she thought about Cole. Could Ned have been right? Was it possible that Cole had had a part in this conspiracy?

If so, G.W. would likely die if he attempted to rescue her. Her chest tightened with fear. She had lost her father. She might have lost Ned. She couldn't bear the thought of losing G.W. too.

Rebecca closed her eyes and tried to think. She fought against the rising panic caused by the knowledge that every hoofbeat brought her closer to where she did not want to go.

Suddenly, a group of riders appeared from behind a stand of gum trees. They pounded toward Rebecca and her captors, weapons drawn. Lem loosened his grip on Rebecca and she could once again breathe freely.

Rebecca's heart almost stopped when she saw Cole. She fixed her eyes on him as though he might disappear if she looked away. Desperately, she wanted to find safety in his arms.

Cole held his rifle pointed at her captors, his eyes narrow slits of anger. His black hair gleamed in the sun. Rebecca recognized the men with him as G.W.'s ranch hands. Their faces were hard and alert, daring any of Rebecca's captors to reach for a weapon.

Jess's horse danced uneasily. Gathering his reins tighter, he faced Cole. "You don't want to do this," he said in an oily tone. "The boss has no liking for you as it is. Don't make it worse."

"It couldn't get worse," Cole said, his voice low and firm.

"You forget where your loyalty ought to lie. Interfering with this woman is going to get you killed."

Cole's jaw tightened. His finger flinched on his rifle. "Let her off the horse real easy." He didn't take his eyes off Jess; his harsh order was for the big man who held Rebecca.

Lem hesitated. Jess reached for his gun. The lightning-fast jerk of Cole's rifle startled Rebecca. Before she could make sense of what had happened, she saw Jess lying on the ground, clutching his injured arm and whimpering.

"Anybody else want to reach for his gun?" Cole asked. The cold look on his face made Rebecca shiver.

He swung to face the man who held Rebecca. "Throw down your gun and let her go."

Rebecca slipped from the saddle as soon as she felt Lem's arms relax. She raced to Cole, who reached down and drew her up to sit behind him on his horse.

Lem slid from his horse and knelt beside Jess. His face filled with indignation as he warned, "The boss's going to hear about this."

"Then you better pick up that low-life on the ground and go tell him," Cole growled as he turned his horse away.

Rebecca held tightly to his waist. She told Cole, "They hurt Ned. He was lying on the porch when I left."

Cole's men formed a rear guard as Rebecca and Cole rode back to the ranch. She glanced over her shoulder to see Jess's men hoist him onto his horse. She wondered about Finley's reaction at having Jess return with a bullet in his arm.

Rebecca took comfort in Cole's closeness and the warmth of his back as she huddled behind him. She was relieved to be safe and to know that Cole had played no part in Andrew's plans. Yet, by helping her, both Cole and G.W. had put themselves in danger. She longed for a safe place where they could all be free of the fear that had become part of their lives. Yet she knew that while Andrew Finley desired herself and her property, none of them were safe.

Rebecca squinted for a view of her house. Tears clouded her vision as anxiety for Ned filled her heart. She pushed away the painful possibility that she would be burying him beside her father.

To her relief, she found Ned slouched on the porch, his

back against the top step. She knelt beside him and asked, "How bad are you hurt?"

Ned rubbed the back of his head. "Just a bump back here. I've had worse."

Rebecca examined the cut from the pistol butt. A stream of blood trickled down the back of his neck. Gingerly, she felt the knot. "Can you stand up?"

Ned staggered as he tried to rise. His shaky legs buckled and Cole caught him, supported him until they reached the kitchen, where he sank into a chair.

Rebecca cleansed the cut with soap and water. She was glad to see the bleeding had stopped. Ned bore her ministrations stoically, wincing as he told them, "I'm embarrassed to admit that they took me by surprise. I woke up with this bump on me head and Rebecca nowhere in sight."

Rebecca shuddered. "Finley sent his men for me. If not for Cole, I'd be his prisoner."

Ned appraised Cole, flinching as Rebecca rinsed away the soap. "How did ye know what happened?"

"Wally saw riders carrying a woman toward Finley's ranch. Since there aren't many women in these parts, so he figured it might be Rebecca and he came for help. Fortunately, we were close by, working on the fence."

Rebecca studied Cole's sober face. "Thank goodness for Wally's sharp eyes. And thank you for coming to my rescue. I owe you so much."

Her heart soared to know that Cole would not have stolen her away from Finley, wounding his foreman, if he were Finley's henchman. She was swept up with relief, as though a high wave had carried her safely to shore.

She remembered her cold treatment of Cole the last time she had seen him, how she'd hoped he hadn't fled the kitchen to hide a guilty conscience. Now that she had proof of her error, her obvious mistrust embarrassed her.

As though he'd read her thoughts, Ned said, "Cole, I've been wrong about ye. I thought ye might have been in with

Finley, trying to force us off this place. But then ye wouldn't have done what ye just did to help Rebecca."

Ned offered his hand. "Will ye accept my apology, lad?"

Cole took Ned's hand. "I will. You can be sure I'll never do anything that would help Finley." His eyes held a smoldering resentment. "He'll force me to kill him someday and I'll welcome the chance." His voice chilled Rebecca to the bone. She swallowed hard.

Ned said simply, "You really hate him, don't ye?"

"More than you can imagine."

Ned flexed his gnarled hands. "Hate's a hard thing to bear. It eats at a man until there's nothing left but the hate."

"In that case, I'll hope for an excuse to rid myself of it soon," Cole replied.

Ned shook his head. His stooped shoulders showed he was too tired to belabor the point. He attempted to push up from the table, and Cole caught him under the arm.

Ned steadied himself against Cole. "The sheep need tending," he said wearily.

Cole shook his head. "Not by you. I'll go with Rebecca and see to them. You spend today resting."

Cole helped Ned to his bed in the lean-to and placed a rifle at his elbow.

Rebecca, left alone in the kitchen, felt a sudden nervous anticipation at the prospect of spending the day with Cole. Her fingers trembled as she tied a lunch bundle for herself and Cole, and another to leave with Ned.

She gave Ned his lunch and then met Cole at the horses. Their fingers brushed as he took the bundle of food and tied it onto the saddle. She caught her breath, her heartbeat quickening from the simple contact.

"Do you think Ned's well enough to stay here alone?" she asked to cover her nervousness.

"He'll be fine if he takes it easy today," Cole replied.

Rebecca swung onto her horse. "I'm truly grateful for what you've done for us. If Ned had been too weak to unpin the sheep today, they would have died without water. Then I would have lost the ranch even if I managed to escape Finley."

"I'm glad I got there before it was too late. You don't deserve such treatment. Nobody does."

Rebecca bit her lip as she saw Cole's face darken with the fury of his bad memories. She watched without comment as he turned to herd the sheep from the pens. She followed behind to keep the stragglers in line as they headed for pasture.

For most of the morning, their work kept them too busy to allow much conversation. When the sheep were at last settled to graze and drink at the shallow stream, Rebecca spread their lunch under a gum tree atop a gentle rise. She nestled onto the cool grass and watched Cole return a stray lamb to its mother.

He finished and swung from his horse with muscular ease. Tying the horse to graze nearby, he joined Rebecca under the tree. She watched him sweep off his hat and set it on the ground. His hair fell boyishly across his forehead. Rebecca could barely resist the urge to brush it tenderly off his face. He had done so much for her. She longed to know whether his actions were inspired by feelings for her or by a desire to thwart Finley.

As she mused, he inspected the cold mutton, muffins, and jelly. His face lit up with a spontaneous grin. "You can do more with a few ingredients than any woman I've ever seen," he said admiringly.

Rebecca returned his smile. "My aunt believed frugality was next to godliness."

Cole's chuckle warmed her heart. "Maybe some good came of your time with her."

Rebecca nodded thoughtfully. "Good can come of any bad situation. I learned a lot about myself and the things I wanted out of life."

Cole regarded her intently, capturing her eyes and holding them with his own. "What do you want, Rebecca?" He spoke her name softly, nearly a caress.

She swallowed hard. For a moment, she could only stare into the depths of his dark eyes and wish her heart could speak her thoughts and give meaning to what words could not express.

He watched her, waiting for her reply. She lowered her eyes and said softly, "The same things most women want. A home, the right person to share it with." Her heart beat so swiftly she was sure he could see the pulse racing in her throat.

"Is G.W. the right person?" His voice held an envy that betrayed his attempt to sound detached.

Her eyes traveled across his face, compelled by the desire to read the emotion behind his question. They lingered on his lips, full and firm. Embarrassed by her attraction, she forced herself to meet his eyes and saw vulnerability in the veiled depths.

She had promised herself she would not entertain another impossible fantasy. It hurt too much when reality broke the spell. She had suffered days of dark misery when she thought he was in Finley's pocket. Today, his actions had cleared him. Her heart rejoiced with the return of her dream. In spite of her intentions, she had fallen for Cole.

Rebecca sighed. Unsure how to answer, she chose caution. "It seems reasonable that G.W. should be the right man. My father wanted me to marry him. But," she added, "hearts don't always cooperate with what is reasonable."

"No. They don't," Cole said simply.

Rebecca dropped her eyes to his strong hands, remembering how they had pulled her onto his horse, rescuing her from danger. When she had sat behind him, clinging to his waist, she'd known the memory would linger in her mind and haunt her dreams.

"I'm sorry I doubted you," she said softly.

"You had a right, though I had hoped since your aunt

treated you badly, you'd understand how I feel about Finley."

She nodded. "I do understand. Deep in my heart I always trusted you."

They finished their lunch in silence. At last Cole said, "I'm still responsible for your father's accident. I fixed the wheel that came off that wagon. I did my best. I don't know why it came off. Still, that will always stand between us." A flicker of pain crossed his face.

Rebecca shook her head vigorously. "No. I don't hold an accident against you."

Cole squinted into the distance, his face pinched with remorse. "I don't understand what happened. I did everything right. I learned from the best wheelwright there is. That's one thing Finley couldn't take from me."

"You learned from him?"

"No. A bloke named Sam fixed wagons for Andrew. He had a limp and couldn't do much riding or tending sheep, but he could repair anything that broke. He was a good man and I spent as much time as I could with him."

"What happened to him?"

"He's still there, if he's alive. Finley hates any kind of weakness and, like I told you, Sam had a limp. Finley criticized Sam, finding nothing but fault in his work, though it was always good. By the time I left, he'd driven Sam to drink."

Rebecca ached with pity for a man she'd never met. "How awful. Why didn't Sam leave?"

"Not much work around for a lame wheelwright."

"I suppose not."

"I intended to study the wheel that came off your father's wagon and see if I could figure out what happened. But Ned had already hauled it back and fixed it. I'll never know what went wrong."

"What's important is that it was an accident."

Cole studied her carefully. "Do you mean that? I never

thought you could forgive me. I thought you'd hate me when you learned the truth."

Rebecca shook her head. "Ned was right. Hate's like a disease. It grows until it ruins your life. We have to forgive for our own good. I learned this truth when I forgave my aunt. It was like a huge weight lifted from my heart."

A scowl darkened Cole's brow. "I don't want to forgive Finley. I can't forget what he did to my mother."

"You don't have to forget. But don't let it make you bitter."

Cole's eyes caressed her face, as though memorizing every curve. "I've never been more scared than I was today. I was afraid I might be too late to save you."

Rebecca caught her lip, hardly daring to acknowledge that the concern in his voice went beyond friendship. Cole gently brushed a stray tendril of hair from her face.

She shivered at his touch and looked deeply into his eyes. Her longing to be loved vied with the fears gained from painful rejections in her past. Running the risk of sounding foolish, she said, "I loved a horse once. It broke my heart to find out it was too wild to ever love me."

"Perhaps it never knew you wanted it," he replied.

"It never let me get close," she said breathlessly.

"Then it was a fool."

He leaned closer. Rebecca's heart pounded with the realization that he was going to kiss her. She closed her eyes as he met her lips gently and tenderly, with a kiss that was soft and sweet. As he drew away she looked up at him, seeing his uncertainty.

She felt lightheaded from the sudden shift in closeness, recognizing the emotion in his eyes as the same fear of rejection that plagued her own heart. Smiling shyly, she nodded at the sheep milling near the tree. "You've given them something to talk about this afternoon."

Cole grinned and relaxed against the thick trunk. "I've

wanted to give them something to talk about since I brought you to your ranch."

"Is that so?" Rebecca asked teasingly.

"Yes."

Rebecca's heart swelled with the knowledge that the attraction she felt was not one-sided. "Perhaps we are living in a fairytale, and you are my knight sent to save me from danger."

Cole nodded, and then became sober. "That plan was nearly spoiled today. Promise you will be extra careful from now on."

Rebecca smiled cheerfully as she got to her feet. "I'll be careful, though you know fairytales always have happy endings."

Cole cast her a doubtful glance as he followed her to their horses.

Chapter nine

For the rest of the day, Cole floated on the sweet assurance of Rebecca's affection. Perhaps she was right about their fairytale. Perhaps they were meant for each other. Yet he could not dislodge the worrisome idea that bad things often happened to people he cared about. And he cared about Rebecca. He knew he could not bear it if he should fail to protect her and harm befell her.

He stayed for supper and checked on Ned before heading home. G.W. met him in the ranch yard before he could dismount. "The men told me what happened. Thanks for taking care of Rebecca. I hate to think of what would have happened if you hadn't been there."

Cole nodded as he turned away. His conscience pricked like a child's carrying a guilty secret. G.W. did not know about the kiss under the tree. Admitting this betrayal to his boss would damage their friendship. Yet to deny his growing attraction to Rebecca would be like having a wound that would not heal. Cole's mind churned with indecision. Any choice he made could end only in pain.

By the time Saturday arrived, Cole wished he had an excuse to escape the poetry reading. How could he sit near Rebecca, listen to her speak, and not let his face show what was growing in his heart? He knew he had to resist the urge to let his feelings be known. For everyone's sake, he had to maintain the iron will he had developed in his youth. Until he could sort out the consequences, he could not declare his intent. It wouldn't be easy.

He washed up and prepared to accompany G.W. Though G.W.'s shoulder had healed enough to allow him to resume most of the tasks around the ranch, his improved health did not remove the threat of Finley, and Cole felt honor-bound to escort him to Kangaroo Flats.

G.W. sat astride his horse, waiting impatiently for Cole. His face had been scrubbed and his hair slicked back. Cole avoided his eyes as he swung onto his own mount.

Perhaps there was no solution that would make everyone happy. G.W. had already waited a long time to find a wife. No matter if Cole had come to love Rebecca. G.W. had been too good a friend for Cole to court her without his blessing.

Rebecca dried the heavy iron skillet and paused at the kitchen window to watch Cole and G.W. ride into the yard. Anticipation mixed with agitation as they dismounted. Cole's kiss had forced her to recognize that the respect she felt for G.W. was not the romantic love that she craved.

It would be hard to tell him the truth—not only for his sake, but also for her own. If she turned G.W., steady and loyal, away and Cole proved as unattainable as the stallion she had once sought to tame, she faced a lonely future.

Rebecca's cowardice nagged at her as she poured coffee into mugs. She assured herself that she needed time to think before making a hasty decision she might regret.

Cole walked into the kitchen, and her heart began its traitorous hammering. She turned her attention to G.W. and smiled. "It's good to see you without a sling on that arm."

He grinned sheepishly. "I'd leave it on to keep your sympathy if it wasn't getting in my way."

She laughed, refreshed by his honesty. "You can still have my sympathy and a cup of coffee."

G.W. reached into his pocket. "I brought you a letter from town. My men picked it up for you."

Rebecca accepted the letter. "It's from Anna! I'm so glad she wrote."

The men sat down with their coffee while Rebecca scanned the letter. "She sends her sympathy on behalf of my father. She says she is settled in town now. I do wish it were safe to invite her for a visit. But as things are . . ." Her voice trailed before she recovered and, not wishing to dampen the mood of the evening, she served the mutton steaks she had fried.

After supper, they settled down, chatting awhile before Rebecca chose a poem. Her eyes were drawn to Cole's face in spite of herself. He seemed to be carefully avoiding her gaze. Yet, when their eyes did meet, his expression of hopeful longing told her he had not forgotten the honest feelings they had shared.

Rebecca chided herself for her distraction and struggled to take her attention off Cole.

The poem she had chosen was an allegory about a father's love. When she finished her reading, her eyes filled with tears at the memory of her own father. She missed him so deeply. Though she had been only a child when they parted, she realized his steady love had prepared her to face the difficulties that had lately filled her life.

G.W.'s moist eyes told her that her reading had evoked similar memories for him. She congratulated herself for introducing the richness of poetry to a man who had never explored such a depth of feeling.

Then she glanced at Cole and all of her self-accolades fled from her mind. Immediately she regretted her choice of poem. His strong jaw looked stone-solid. His dark eyes were downcast and full of the bitterness he felt toward Finley and the guilt he bore for her father's death.

Rebecca felt a sense of relief when the evening ended and the two men departed. Though she didn't think G.W. had been aware of the tension hanging in the air, she had been keenly aware of it. She realized that even if she could convince Cole of her forgiveness, he could not forgive himself. Would the ghosts from his past always hover between them?

Cole was silent on the ride home. Though Rebecca had forgiven him, he suffered a pang of guilt every time someone mentioned Roger's name. Each time he saw Rebecca's tears for her father, the weight of his remorse settled in his chest.

Oblivious to Cole's bleak mood, G.W. chatted buoyantly about his plans. "I think this poetry is winning her over. Do you think I should bring up marrying again? I don't want to rush her, but she's so pretty that it's hard to wait." He sighed good-naturedly and said, "You'd stand up at our wedding, wouldn't you? She'll want Ned to give her away."

Cole could hardly think of anywhere that he'd rather not be. Yet he lacked an excuse to decline. "Sure. I'd stand with you," he said woodenly.

"Wouldn't be the same if you didn't."

Cole glanced at G.W. His round face was lit by the pale moonlight.

G.W. grinned. "You're a loyal mate. You kept things running after I was shot. And, if it weren't for you, Finley would have taken Rebecca. I couldn't have stood the way he would have treated her."

Cole swallowed hard. He'd made a mess of things. He'd gone behind his best mate's back and tempted the heart of the girl he loved. Her feelings for him might keep her from marrying G.W. Yet Cole knew he himself fell short of what Rebecca deserved. The thought was as unsettling as stepping on a snake and waiting for the bite. He just hoped he was the only one who would get hurt.

He turned his face to the wisp of clouds that skirted the moon, as though he might find a way out of this mess. He found no answer.

He lay awake late into the night, fighting his feelings. When he finally fell asleep, he had not succeeded in quelling his desire to be with Rebecca again. He longed to sit under a tree and share his thoughts and feelings with her. He longed to touch her soft lips with his own. For G.W.'s sake, as well as his own, he wished it were not true. He had not planned or desired for this to happen. Yet he could no more deny his deepening affection than deny that the yellow sun rose each day in the sky.

Wally came late the next morning to watch the sheep while Cole worked on the fence. "Everything okay at Kangaroo Flats?" Cole asked.

Wally grinned broadly. "Your missy gave me a sheep for bringing you to her rescue. It made good stew."

Cole eyed him. "Better not call her my missy."

"Why? She cares for you."

Cole wiped his brow. "It's not that simple. G.W. wants to marry her."

Wally shook his head. "No matter."

Cole glanced up sharply. "What do you mean, 'no matter'?"

"She wants you."

Cole sighed, wishing life were as simple as Wally made it sound. "So now you're an expert on love? Go watch the sheep."

Wally trotted off, leaving Cole to consider his pronouncement.

Rebecca shivered at the boldness of her plan to herd her sheep to the far pasture so she could carry her lunch over to eat with Cole. She had not been able to read Ned's reaction to her idea. Nonetheless, she cast her reserve aside with the knowledge that in a few days, the migrant workers would arrive for shearing season and Cole would put aside the fence project until the shearing was finished.

It took most of the morning to get the sheep to pasture. It was nearly noon when they were settled for the afternoon grazing. Ned settled down with his own lunch, his broad-brimmed hat hiding his face. "You do your visiting," he said. "I'll watch the sheep."

Rebecca's heart beat in rapid rhythm as she rode over with her lunch. The delight in Cole's eyes made up for the exertion of riding in the noon heat.

"I decided you have better shade for a picnic," she said.

Cole raised his brows and glanced around. "Where?"

Rebecca rapidly scanned the trees and pointed to a gum with spreading branches. "There."

Cole grinned. "There's shadier trees where you left your sheep."

Rebecca reveled in the warmth of his smile. Still, she felt her cheeks flush as she tossed her head and strolled toward the tree. "Then we'll say I've come on a mission of goodwill."

They settled under the branches and assuaged their parched throats with swallows from their canteens. Cole's work crew scattered under the remaining trees to eat their noon rations. Wally grinned at them from a grove of bushy berries that had stained his teeth a festive blue.

Cole studied her carefully, a tentative smile on his lips. "Goodwill, huh?"

Rebecca smiled sweetly. "That's right."

"I was hoping you'd come to see me." His grin was obvious now.

"I did," Rebecca admitted softly. "I needed an excuse."

He took her hand, holding it gently in his long, sun-browned fingers. "You don't need an excuse. I've always enjoyed your company."

She smiled. "You had a funny way of showing it. You tried to send me back to Sydney."

Cole's eyes shadowed with the memory. "I thought the only way to prevent you from hating me was to convince you to leave before you learned the truth."

She gave his hand a gentle squeeze. "It seems you were wrong."

He looked deeply into her eyes. "You can't know how much I want to believe that."

She met his gaze. "Then believe it, because it's the truth."

Rebecca hardly tasted her lunch as she and Cole shared a private cocoon of shade. A small gray pigeon strutted nearby, clucking and bowing and puffing his throat feathers to impress a female in the tree.

Rebecca laughed at the little bird. "Do you know any tricks to impress me?" she asked Cole.

He raised an eyebrow. "I have no interest in a contest." Pointing at her, he said, "You, little bird, will have to make your own choice."

The look in his eyes made Rebecca fear he might be referring to G.W.'s plan, a matter she did not want to discuss. She changed the subject. "Will you be going to Sydney with the wool?"

"Always do, though I don't welcome the long trip."

She nodded. "Father used to leave Ned in charge while he made the trip. When Mother and I moved, he tried to see us, but Aunt Abigail wouldn't let him."

Cole's eyes drifted to her sheep. "Have you given any thought to getting your wool to market? You don't belong on a sheep drive and it's too dangerous for you to send Ned and stay alone at your ranch. We could load your wagon and take your wool with us."

She nodded. "That would certainly help. I'd pay for the extra trouble, of course."

He started to speak, and then changed his mind. "You can work that out with G.W."

She saw him glance at the sun, then at his waiting project. Reluctantly, she rose. "I'd better let you get back to work."

"Will you come tomorrow?"

"Do you promise to believe my excuse?"

"Of course." He nodded solemnly and then grinned.

"Then I'll be back."

For the next three days, Rebecca joined Cole for lunch under their tree. On the fourth day, she arrived to find the fence work abandoned. The shearing crew had arrived. They would come to her pens next. Then Cole would leave to take the wool. The month they would spend apart stretched interminably before her.

Their intimate time together had left Rebecca feeling a new depth of compatibility. She felt complete in his presence, as though she'd discovered a part of herself that had been missing. She could not feel whole again until he returned.

They brought the sheep in early that day. Wally watched over the pens while Ned and Rebecca took the wagon to town to buy the extra supplies they would need when the shearing crew arrived. They arrived in late afternoon, as the shadows of the buildings stretched to meet each other in the street.

Walter Adams, who owned the dry goods store, was a stout, balding man given to chatter. He wasted no time informing Rebecca of the arrival of a letter.

"The coach brought it yesterday. I said I would hold it here until you came to town."

Rebecca studied the curved letters of her name, written in unfamiliar writing. It was from Sydney, but not from her aunt. She opened the envelope slowly.

It contained a note from a solicitor, written on expensive, fine-grained paper.

Wordlessly, she handed it to Ned. "It says my aunt has

died. I'm to come to Sydney at once, or send a note with someone authorizing them to act in my behalf."

Ned scanned the letter and handed it back. "Yer not thinking of going, are ye?"

She shook her head. "No. I suppose the solicitor expects me to see to the sale of her house. It won't fetch much—she never spent a farthing to keep it up. Still, I have to give him some sort of an answer."

"Cole will be taking wool to Sydney soon. Ye could ask him to pay a visit on the fellow."

Rebecca considered the suggestion. "I don't want to burden anyone. Maybe I'll ask if he minds. He can do whatever seems reasonable about the house."

She fingered the edge of the smooth paper. "I hope my aunt hasn't left any debt. The sale of our wool will give us just enough to meet our needs for the year. There won't be anything left over."

The possibility of debt worried her as she selected the needed supplies, yet she felt grateful for the suggestion that Cole might be willing to handle the meeting with the solicitor. The thought of returning to Sydney for any reason gave her a hollow feeling inside.

She deposited a box of groceries into the wagon and then went back inside to find Ned chatting with Walter.

"I'm going to look for my friend, Anna, and pay her a visit while I'm in town."

Walter had a fondness for cigars, and Rebecca preferred the fresh outside air to the acrid odor of the store. She walked along the street, scanning the rows of weathered buildings lining the boardwalk. After spending years among the conveniences of Sydney, she realized how little she missed the trappings of town.

A rowdy group of men sauntered toward the saloon. From behind the doors, the tinny sound of an off-key piano drifted into the street. Nearby, a young woman sat alone in a wagon. Rebecca squinted at her profile. As though she sensed Rebecca's curious gaze, the woman turned and Rebecca recognized Anna.

Hungry for feminine conversation, Rebecca hurried over, lifting her skirt above the dusty street. "Anna? I was just coming to see you. I have so much to tell you. I wrote it in a letter, but now I have come to town." She offered Anna her hand.

Anna's eyes softened with recognition. She extended her slim pale hand. "I was so sorry about your father. You were so excited about seeing him again."

Rebecca nodded. "So much has happened since then. I do hope we will be able to talk." She eyed the wagon. "Are you going away?"

Anna's eyes widened with anticipation. "I am. I have been invited to make my home with a man of property. Whatever you may think of that, it's better than the saloon." Her eyes and tone dared Rebecca to object.

Ignoring the challenge, Rebecca said, "I'm happy for you. Where will you be going?"

"I'm going to Andrew Finley's ranch. You've probably heard of it. I'm going as soon as he's ready." She nodded toward the bar.

Rebecca felt the breath squeeze from her lungs as she gasped, "You can't be serious. He is the very man who has tried to murder my friend and kidnap me for the sake of my ranch. He is a cruel and vicious man. Please, Anna, you can ask his stepson how he treated his last wife."

Anna's eyes grew huge and round. Rebecca pulled at her sleeve. "Quick, you must get out of the wagon!"

Anna sat as though in a stupor, frozen by indecision, when Finley's bulky frame emerged from the bar. The memory of their last meeting chilled Rebecca's blood as he fixed her with a cold stare.

He loomed over her before she could retreat. "I see you've met the lucky lady. It could have been you. You could have left that stinking shack you call home. It's too late now. I'll find another way to get what I want from you."

Rebecca melted against the wagon as he brushed past, so close she could smell the rum on his breath.

Anna's sudden pallor betrayed her fear. Rebecca grasped the opportunity and cried, "Anna, you don't have to do this! You can stay with me at my place."

Finley clutched Anna's arm, holding her in her seat, as he took up the reins and snorted, "No one with any sense would choose that pigsty."

The wagon jolted as his rough command set the horses in motion. A cry of protest died in Rebecca's throat, replaced by a sinking feeling in her stomach. A last look at Anna's frightened face, turned toward her, seared into her memory as Finley drove her away.

Her feet felt leaden as she trudged back down the street. She approached her own wagon as Ned set a sturdy box onto its floor and then paused to study her.

"Yer white as a sheet. Who were ye watching drive away?" he asked.

Rebecca settled into the wagon and explained what had happened.

"My friend has gone away with Andrew Finley. If I had had a few more minutes with her, I could have convinced her to change her mind. Now I don't know what to do," she lamented. "If it was anyone but him, I could pay a friendly visit and see how she was doing."

Ned nodded in agreement. "Ye can't do that. I suppose there's nothing a body can do but hope for the best."

Seeing the truth in his statement, Rebecca stewed with worry until the Saturday night visit with Cole and G.W. She had not been able to get Anna off her mind for days. When she told the men what had happened, G.W. sputtered, "There must be something we can do."

"She went of her own will," Ned reminded them.

Cole's eyes smoldered with anger. "She didn't know

what she was getting into. By now, she'll be sorry." He reached for his hat.

"Where are you going?" Rebecca cried.

"To see if I can get past Finley's men to the main house."

Rebecca reached for his arm, her eyes wide with fear. "You can't be serious. He would love an excuse to kill you."

G.W. nodded. "She's right, Cole. You can't go alone."

Ned studied Cole, his sharp eyes reading the young man's tortured face. "She's not yer mother, Cole. She may not want to be rescued."

G.W. leaned forward, his round face thoughtful. "That's true. She's not asked for our help. If she does, we'll go together."

Defeated, Cole sank back into his chair. He ran his long fingers through his thick hair as he drew a deep, resigned breath. "You're right. Still, I can't help thinking that by now she must regret her decision. I can't abide the thought of any woman suffering at the hands of that snake."

As Cole withdrew into his own thoughts, Rebecca fought the urge to reach out and stroke his troubled brow. She longed to assure him that he would someday find relief from his painful past.

When the evening ended, she caught Cole's arm as he was leaving. "Promise you won't do anything rash that will get you killed," she begged.

He looked into her pleading eyes and felt his heart twist with the knowledge that she truly cared. He touched her face, tenderly brushing back a lock of hair. "I won't."

G.W. called to him from the yard.

Cole tensed and quickly withdrew his finger from Rebecca's satiny cheek. He turned away quickly, frustrated that he felt like a guilty schoolboy stealing her affection behind G.W.'s back.

He had not dared to believe that Rebecca could care for him. Now that he knew she did, he longed for the freedom to openly express his feelings. Yet Rebecca had not told G.W. how she felt. Her hesitancy to choose between them disturbed him. Did her hesitation to commit her feelings mean that she might yet change her mind?

Chapter ten

Rebecca was swept up in a sense of nostalgia when the migrant shearing crew arrived. It had been years since she'd watched them wrestle the sheep into the creek for a scrub with soft brown soap and then a rinse. To her childish delight, the sheep had emerged white as clouds. After the sheep dried, the pens echoed with bleating as brawny men clamped each animal by the forelegs and expertly removed the heavy curly coats.

She would have no time to watch them now. Her time was consumed by duties in the kitchen. She remembered her mother complaining that the men ate like a swarm of locusts. Hard labor produced large appetites and massive meals involved massive clean-ups. Rebecca worked in an endless cycle of cooking from dawn to dusk to feed the stomachs of nine hungry men.

The days had been growing progressively warmer, bringing swarms of flies that crept over her flesh. She brushed them away in annoyance as she chopped mutton for the afternoon stew. The flies returned so quickly that she soon gave up the effort of shooing them away.

The long days in the kitchen tried her patience, as she had always preferred the outdoors to domestic activities.

Even the direct rays of the scorching sun would be favorable to the stifling heat of the kitchen. She reminded herself that the shearing would soon end and steeled herself to her tasks. Each evening, she admired the increasing piles of wool that lay graded, baled, and wrapped in jute.

Ned sat with Rebecca at twilight after the second day and informed her of the progress. "They're an efficient group of blokes. They should be done tomorrow."

Rebecca stretched her sore muscles and sighed. "I won't be sorry to see them go."

As Ned predicted, the men finished the next morning and collected their wages. After they headed out to their next job, Rebecca scanned the sky with a wary eye. Gray thunderheads congregated like armies assembling for an assault. She frowned at the possibility of a storm. Any other time, rain would be a welcome relief to the heat. But dampness would be a threat to the health of her newly shorn sheep.

By lunchtime, the sky had not produced rain. Rebecca packed a lunch and drove the freshly shorn sheep to where Ned tended the rest of the flock. Then, just after lunch, large drops of rain began to fall. Rebecca cringed at the possibility of losing sheep. She mounted her horse and was debating the best spot to seek shelter when she was startled to see a bay horse carrying a slumped rider ambling toward her.

She squinted into the rain. Her experiences with Finley prompted her to be cautious. It could be a trick; someone pretending injury to get close enough to fire a shot. Ned motioned her to stay with the sheep as he drew his pistol and edged his horse forward to get a better look.

Rebecca watched the rider sway, barely able to keep in the saddle, and decided he was either ill or exhausted. Ned reached the rider and cried out in dismay. Rebecca cantered out to join them, and then drew her horse to an abrupt halt, shocked by the sight of the battered girl clinging to the horse.

Anna's dark hair clung damply to her head. A purple bruise encircled one swollen eye and an angry gash stretched from the corner of her mouth.

"I remembered what you told me. You told me I could come to you," Anna murmured, barely moving her painful lips.

Tears filled Rebecca's eyes. "I remember. Do you think you can stay in the saddle if I lead your horse?"

Anna nodded. Yet keeping the injured girl in the saddle meant slow progress. Ned rode ahead to put the sheep in the sheds, then came back to help.

"Yer both getting soaked. Lead my horse and I'll climb behind Anna and hold 'er on. We can get her out of the rain quicker."

Anna seemed barely conscious when they reached the house. Ned lifted her from the saddle and helped Rebecca get her to a chair in the kitchen. He tended to the horses while Rebecca wrapped Anna in a light blanket and began to clean her face.

Anna slumped in the chair, her eyes dull. Rebecca's mind reeled with worry as she dabbed away the crusted blood at the corner of Anna's mouth. "I need to know how badly you're hurt. Do you think you have any broken bones?"

Anna drew a slow breath as she focused on Rebecca's face. "I don't think he broke any bones. He caught me packing to leave him. He thought he beat me too bad for me to go, but I was determined to get away."

Ned walked into the kitchen, his face full of concern. "How is she?"

"I think the damage will heal. We ought to get her to bed."

When Anna had been dried off and carefully laid in Rebecca's bed, Rebecca made coffee. She sat at the table with Ned. Her hand shook as she lifted her cup, eyes filling with tears. "I still remember her face when he drove her away.

I told her not to go. I told her she could come here, but I was too late."

Ned's frown deepened. "Did Finley hear yer invitation?"

Rebecca nodded. "I suppose he did."

"Then he'll be looking for 'er. I know she's in a bad way, but we've got to move 'er before he gets here."

The truth of his words registered in Rebecca's mind. He was right. Finley would come looking. If he found Anna here, he would think it good cause to murder all of them.

"Where should we take her?"

He rubbed his grizzled beard. "It's too far to town and I don't know if anyone would take 'er in. We best go to G.W.'s place."

Rebecca nodded. "I'll get Anna while you saddle the horses."

She roused Anna from a deep sleep. "I know you want to rest, but we have to move so that he doesn't find you."

Anna's eyes widened with alarm. She sat up, gasping with the pain caused by her effort. Rebecca laid a comforting hand on her shoulder. "He's not here, but he may come. We're taking you over to G.W. Sanders's ranch. Finley will have a hard time forcing his way in there."

Anna nodded. She let Rebecca dress her and lead her outside to the horses. Ned helped her onto his horse and climbed up behind her. "I sent the horse she took from Finley home. We don't want him to accuse anyone of being a horse thief."

The rain had stopped. The storm had drained the sky of color, leaving it an anemic shade of blue. Rebecca felt as drained as it looked. Yet her tense muscles would not allow her to relax. She scanned the treeline bordering Finley's ranch and wondered when he would discover Anna's absence. Perhaps he was already on their trail. Anna's weak condition would slow them down. If Finley spotted them, they would stand no chance of escaping him.

Her tension eased when they rode into G.W.'s ranch

yard. With Cole and G.W., they would find shelter and protection.

The smell of stew drifted from the open kitchen windows. Most of the men were returning for a dinner break. G.W. and Cole rode into the yard just as Ned swung from his horse.

The men's smiles of pleasure at receiving company faded when they caught sight of Anna's bruised face. G.W. swung from his horse and said, "I'll take her inside."

He lifted the girl gently from her horse as Ned followed behind.

Rebecca sat her mount, troubled by the rigid look on Cole's face. His eyes burned with fury. Without a word, he wheeled his horse around and took off toward the gate.

Fear seized Rebecca. The unreasoning hatred she'd seen in his eyes filled her heart with ice. She had to stop him before he threw his life away at Finley's hands.

Cole allowed himself to vent his rage in a few minutes of hard riding. Then, as his mind cleared, he saw the need to devise a plan. The best he could hope for by shooting his way onto Finley's ranch would be to kill a few hands. No doubt he would also be killed. His death would serve no purpose if Finley would live to torment other innocent victims who crossed his path. If he wanted to kill Finley, he would have to think clearly.

He slowed his horse to give himself time to think, and he realized he was being followed. He whipped his head around to see Rebecca riding at breakneck speed.

She arrived breathless, her hair in windblown disarray. She pulled her horse to a stop directly beside him, she cried, "I won't let you do anything foolish. I'll follow you wherever you go."

"Did you really think I'd ride straight into gunfire?" Cole asked, touched by her concern for him. "I'll set a watch and wait for Finley to come looking for his woman. Then I'll challenge him."

She grasped his arm. "And if he brings his men? Anna's safe now. How will it help her to get yourself killed?"

"You don't know how it feels to sit by and watch him maim another victim. It's like having my heart seared by a brand." He banged a balled fist against his chest. "Someone has to stop him."

Rebecca shook her head. "Not you. Not like this."

"So he gets away with it?" Cole asked coldly.

Rebecca bit her lip, watching him closely. "No one gets away with such evil in the long run. And I don't want to lose you."

The depth of her blue eyes held Cole spellbound. He felt his anger shift to longing, and leaned toward her. In a gesture of possession, he pulled her against him. Her eyes widened, yet she did not resist as he claimed her mouth in a gentle kiss. Driven by a suppressed longing for closeness to another human being, he enjoyed the softness of her lips until she slowly pulled away.

"I'm sorry," he said, knowing it wasn't true.

Her cheeks were flushed a soft shade of rose. "I'm not. But I think we'd better get back before someone comes looking."

Her reasonable words brought him back to his senses. For everyone's sake, he had to bring his wayward emotions under control. Before they'd gone far, G.W. appeared. His anxious frown relaxed when he saw them.

"I'm glad you stopped him, Rebecca. I was worried Cole had taken leave of his senses."

Cole shook his head. "I needed to ride hard to take the edge off my anger."

G.W. nodded. "I understand. That poor girl didn't deserve to be beat."

Cole sighed. "All the more reason for him to beat her. He doesn't respect anyone who isn't as much of a snake as he is. Think of what he did to Sam. He tormented Sam until he became a drunken shell of a man."

"Maybe he'll find an escape someday, like Anna has," Rebecca said.

She checked on Anna when they returned to the ranch. Anna slept deeply, her dark hair spilled across the pillow. Rebecca paused in the doorway, filled with pity for the homeless girl. She hoped the future would be kinder than the past.

At supper, G.W. said, "You and Ned better stay here tonight. It won't be safe at your place. You can have my room. We'll sleep in the bunkhouse and set a watch at the gate."

Ned nodded. "I'll go in the morning to check on the sheep."

"Wally can tell us if you had any visitors during the night," Cole said.

Rebecca prepared a late dinner tray for Anna, intending to wake her if need be to encourage her to eat and keep up her strength. As she carried the tray into the hall, the sound of sobbing told her that Anna was already awake. She set the tray on the dresser and sat on the edge of the bed, resting a gentle hand on Anna's shaking shoulder.

"You'll heal. In a few days, all the bruises will be gone," she said, thinking the girl was distraught at her shattered looks.

Anna shook her head. Tears pooled in her dark eyes. "Do you really think I care about that? I've been beaten before. Maybe you can't understand, but I've always wanted a man to be my own and a house to take care of. Maybe children."

She paused, too choked to continue. Rebecca patted her shoulder. "I do understand."

Anna wiped her eyes. "I thought I'd finally found it. I wanted to be good to Andrew. Then, he'd let me stay and I'd have a real home. But he's the meanest man I've ever met. I don't think I'll ever find my dream."

She collapsed again, overcome by another bout of tears.

"That's not true. You will find your dream," Rebecca said, her voice soothing.

The disconsolate look in Anna's eyes told Rebecca it was going to be hard to convince her to have hope for her future. She coaxed Anna into eating a little food, and then left her to rest.

Later, when the men had gone to the bunkhouse, Rebecca lay in G.W.'s room and studied the simple, bachelor starkness. Though the furniture was handsome and solid, the floors were bare and no curtains softened the windows. The room could surely use a woman's touch.

She smiled, surprised at herself—she'd never noticed such things before. She blushed to admit the cause of this attack of domesticity, remembering the warmth of Cole's lips, the hunger she'd sensed in his touch. He loved her. And she loved him and longed to fix up a home for him. Next thing she knew, she'd be hooking rugs and sewing curtains.

Rebecca wondered if her mother had felt the same desire in the early days of her marriage. By the time she was old enough to remember, her mother had seemed unhappy in her household tasks. Perhaps her mother had not loved her father the way Rebecca was beginning to love Cole. It was like honey, intoxicating her senses with its sweet taste. But was their love doomed to tragedy, if Cole insisted on facing Finley? She swallowed hard, forcing herself to think of Anna instead. Somehow they must convince her that the sordid life she had lived was not her only choice.

Rebecca awoke in the middle of the night to hear raised voices outside the bunkhouse. She leaped out of bed and dashed to the window, fearing that Finley had evaded their guard and come for Anna. Yet moonlight revealed only a small group of men gathered around a solitary figure.

Perplexed, she pulled a light wrap around her shoulders and headed for the door. She met Anna in the hallway.

Even in the dim light, Rebecca could see that Anna's eyes were huge and round.

"It's Andrew. He's come for me." Fear filled her voice.

"No. I looked out. It's not Andrew. Go back to bed and I'll find out what's going on."

Anna had spent what little energy she possessed in dragging herself out of bed. Now that she knew she was not in imminent danger, she sagged against the wall, too weak to walk.

Rebecca helped her return to bed, and then hurried outside. The men were still talking. When Ned spotted her, he detached himself from the group and strode to meet her.

"Bad news. Wally said Finley came looking for Anna. When he didn't find anybody about, he had his men set fire to the house, and the sheds, too. We would have lost the wool if Wally hadn't managed to put the fire out. To save the wool, he had to let the house burn. It's gone, lass."

Rebecca stared at him in shock. Her numb mind noticed only that Ned's face looked old and tired in the moonlight. Then, as his words slowly sunk in, she felt her knees grow weak. She had slept each night of her treasured childhood in the bedroom of that beloved house. And now it was gone. Tears filled her eyes.

G.W. approached, and cautiously patted her shoulder. "You can stay here as long as you like. Anna will need to rest for awhile. She could use a woman to care for her until she heals. Then, if you decide to rebuild, some of the men can help after they take the wool to Sydney."

Rebecca bit her lip. Remaining here as G.W.'s long-term guest would be awkward. No doubt he still hoped she would choose to stay as his wife. Still, she couldn't think of another solution to her current dilemma.

She brushed away tears and nodded. "I'd be grateful for your help."

Rebecca followed the men into the kitchen and accepted

a steaming cup of Davies's coffee. Though the room wasn't cold, she shivered uncontrollably as she sank into a chair.

She sensed Cole watching her and glanced at him through tear-laden lashes. His eyes revealed the pain he felt for her loss. She longed to fly into his arms for comfort. Locked in his strong embrace, she would be able to stop trembling. Yet she dared not affront G.W. by such unexpected behavior.

Oblivious, G.W. said, "We could count your sheep and pen them with mine for awhile. It would be safer. I hate to think what Finley might do next."

Ned rubbed his grizzled chin as he told Rebecca, "It's a good idea. During the daytime, they could expand onto yer land for water for grazing, and then drive all of them here at night. And while I'm not tending sheep, I could drive our wool to Sydney and spare G.W. an extra man."

G.W.'s kind heart touched the core of Rebecca's misery. She chose her words carefully. "I'd be pleased to accept your hospitality and your offer to help me rebuild after the men return. But only if you're sure it won't put you to too much trouble."

"Trouble? I would be pleased. I'll have to warn you that I intend to try and convince you not to rebuild at all. I want you to marry me and stay here."

Rebecca drew a sharp breath. Now that G.W. had announced his intentions in front of witnesses, his words hung in the air as though he awaited a reply. She felt Cole's eyes imploring her to be honest. Yet her mouth refused to form the words to voice her commitment. Feeling like a coward, she avoided Cole's eyes and said instead, "I shouldn't like to feel obligated to marriage by your hospitality."

G.W. shook his head. "And you wouldn't be. The offer of my home isn't accompanied by a commitment to marry. I only hope that will be the outcome."

Rebecca swallowed hard, sensing Cole's tension. She wanted him with all her heart. How could she make him understand her difficulty? She couldn't acknowledge her love until she could be sure his love for her was stronger than his hatred for Finley.

She flinched as Cole turned abruptly and left the room. So much had happened in the last hour. She'd entered a valley of uncertainty in which she could only stumble blindly, hoping for a light at the end. If only she could crawl off and hide from the feelings of confusion that threatened to overwhelm her.

Her heart felt leaden when she finally returned to bed. Her home and possessions were gone, her relationship with Cole damaged. She sighed and buried her head in her pillow to stem the tears of self-pity that streamed from her eyes.

Rebecca awoke early with a pulsing headache. She threw aside the sheet and swung her bare feet to the floor, narrowly missing a brown beetle that scurried under the bed.

The promise of fresh air drew her to the window. The earth smelled of dampness from yesterday's rain. Streaks of clouds swirled across the sky, as though painted by a giant's hand, as the golden sun peeked above the horizon.

Cole stood alone on the corral. His horse whinnied and came forward to be rewarded with an affectionate rub on the nose.

Rebecca's heart beat quickly. She had to find a way to make Cole understand her dilemma. She stood frozen at the window until her desire to speak to him outweighed the uncertainty of what she would say. As she dressed, she remembered the letter she'd written giving Cole permission to attend to her affairs in Sydney. She had slipped it into her pocket yesterday morning.

She retrieved the letter and slipped out to the paddock. Though she heard the men stirring in the bunkhouse, Cole was still alone when she arrived, breathless, to face his inscrutable dark eyes. She took a deep breath and said,

"I've no right to ask, but I'm wondering if you could see to some business for me in Sydney."

He raised an eyebrow and waited for her to continue.

"I received a letter from a solicitor telling me my aunt has died. He asked me to come and, if I could not, to send someone to come in my place. I suppose he needs permission to sell the house. There may be debts to be paid."

Cole glanced at the folded paper. Rebecca bit her lip, willing her hand to stop shaking.

"This gives my permission," she explained.

Cole accepted the paper. "I'd be glad to see to this for you. I'd offer you my sympathy about your aunt, but I know you weren't very close."

Rebecca was surprised by the sentiment that gripped her heart. Tears clouded her eyes. "I'm sorry it ended this way. I wish my aunt and I could have been close."

Cole nodded. "And what will you do while I'm gone?"

"I'll tend to Anna and try to find a way to help out. I hate being a burden to G.W. again."

He lifted the saddle from the corral and placed it on the horse. "He didn't sound like he thinks you're a burden. Will I return to find you've become Mrs. Sanders?"

"No." She looked away. "There's a lot to consider in a serious relationship, Cole. My father was a stable man like G.W. He was committed to our family. My mother was not. She let her emotions drive her and, after awhile, she left him."

"You think I would leave you?"

She bit her lip. Her stomach twisted into a painful knot. "No. But your hatred for Finley frightens me. I want to be your wife, not your widow, Cole. And if you kill him for revenge, what kind of man will that make you?"

"So you might marry G.W. even though you know I love you and you love me?"

Tears dampened her lashes. "No. I'll never marry unless it's for love."

"We have love. Can't you marry me and accept me like I am?"

She wiped away the tears. "I do accept you. And I can't help loving you. But I can't marry you until you promise me that you won't throw your life away for the sake of vengeance."

A clamor of voices preceded the men who spilled from the bunkhouse. Rebecca turned from Cole and headed for the house before anyone could notice her damp cheeks. At the porch, she paused and watched him swing into his saddle. As he rode away, she wondered if Finley's existence would continue to keep them apart.

Chapter eleven

Cole plodded his horse toward Kangaroo Flats to help Ned drive Rebecca's flock to join G.W.'s larger herd. He welcomed the time alone to think. Bitterness rose like a sour taste in his throat. Rebecca wanted him to forgive Finley. She had made it clear that he would have to make peace with his past in order to win her hand. Yet, he could not respect himself if he backed down from the vow he had made to avenge his mother's death. And it was his honesty on this account that made Rebecca hesitate to place her affection with him.

He grimaced at the sound of a kookaburra's laughter. It seemed to mock his ill humor. Rebecca defied the physical solutions that usually worked to solve his difficulties. In a brawl, he could use his fists. With a broken wagon, he could break his back under the sweltering sun to put it right. But none of these skills prepared him to deal with a matter of the heart.

He was no closer to an answer when he spotted Ned working near the burned-out ruins of his home, driving sheep from the pens to count and prepare them for a tedious day of grazing and walking. Cole grimaced at the sight of the charred ground, all that remained of the wooden structure. The blackened remains of the sink and stove stood alone, stripped of the walls that had once surrounded them.

When he reached Ned, the old man said, "Got two sheep dying and six more sick. There's not much we can do for them, so we better get the others to dry pasture."

Cole waved his hat in warning toward a dingo that kept its distance as he watched the sheep. The unfinished stretch of fence lay abandoned near the border of the ranches. It was not likely to be finished for another month. Guarding Ned and these sheep would take the entire day. With the journey to Sydney starting early the next morning, the work on the fence would have to wait until he returned.

In the meantime, the helpless sheep, along with Anna and Rebecca, would have to rely on their human protectors. If Cole or the other men let down their guard for even a moment, they could lose everything they held dear. This need for constant vigilance filled him with anger. The world was filled with stray lambs for whom predators lurked, waiting for the chance to devour their prey.

He went after a small lamb that had wandered from the flock. He felt tired of his role as protector. It was a heavy responsibility, his past failures lay heavily on his heart.

He glanced up to see the dingo waiting behind the cover of a gum tree. He knew from experience that one of the lambs would likely become dinner for the persistent hunter before the end of the day.

Rebecca knocked on Anna's door. When she heard no reply, she peeked inside. The girl lay facing the window. Her eyes were open, yet she did not acknowledge Rebecca's presence.

"I've come to see how you feel," Rebecca said softly.

The purple bruises that encircled Anna's eyes made her look all the more forlorn as she turned toward Rebecca. "I wish he'd killed me, you know."

Rebecca stared, stunned by her words. Recovering her

wits, she perched on the edge of the bed. "You don't mean that."

"Yes, I do. What's left for me to do? Go back to the saloon? I don't want to go back." Tears flowed down Anna's cheeks, dampening the edge of the pillow.

Rebecca patted her arm "You won't go back there, ever. G.W. insists that you stay here until you're well. Then, we'll think of something. I promise."

Anna smiled. "You've been good to me. It's nice to have a friend. I'm sorry about your house. It's my fault for going to you."

Rebecca shook her head. "No. Finley only wanted an excuse. He would have found another reason."

Anna edged herself up. Her eyes grew wide. "He's a monster. I would never have escaped if one of the men hadn't put me on a horse when no one was around."

"Who helped you?"

"A man named Sam."

Rebecca pulse jumped. "I've heard about him."

Anna's eyes opened even wider. "How?"

"Cole described him."

Anna clutched the edge of Rebecca's sleeve. "Please, you can't tell anyone. Andrew will kill him if he finds out he helped me escape."

Rebecca nodded. "I won't tell anyone except Cole. He'll want to know his old friend is still alive."

Anna sank back, drained of energy. "I feel so weak. As soon as I'm well, I'll pay everyone back for their kindness."

Rebecca stood. "Right now, you need some breakfast to build up your strength."

She brought Anna a breakfast tray, then spent the rest of the morning collecting food and other provisions Ned would need on the trip to Sydney. Though G.W. had insisted on donating the items, Rebecca kept count so she could pay him back after the sale of her wool.

At lunchtime, she returned to check on Anna. Though

Anna's cheeks were very pale, she sat up in bed, combing her fingers through her tangled hair.

"If you're feeling up to it, you should join G.W and me for lunch."

Anna's eyelids lowered in dismay. "I can't bear to have a man see me like this," she said sadly.

"G.W will be our only company and he won't mind. He was shot through the shoulder a few weeks ago and had to put aside his pride while it healed. Besides, your bruises are fading. You look quite presentable."

As she brushed Anna's hair, Rebecca's thoughts drifted to Cole. All morning she had listened for the sound of his return.

Three weeks, she told herself. It would be at least three weeks before Cole returned from Sydney, perhaps longer if the roads were muddy. It seemed an eternity.

She knew she should stop longing to spend every moment in his presence. Their relationship might yet bring them only pain. Yet, she had told him the truth. And whatever the price, she could not help loving him.

At last Rebecca set aside the brush. "You look fine. You can't sit in this room forever. You're coming to lunch."

Anna examined her face closely in the mirror. She ran a finger along her puffy lip. The bruises on her face, though waning, were still evident.

"I look awful," she proclaimed.

Rebecca grasped Anna's elbow and urged her to her feet. Anna sighed reluctantly, but allowed herself to be led from the room.

G.W waited at the table. He rose, smiling broadly, as they joined him. "Not many men in these parts get to have the company of two lovely ladies."

Anna stiffened at his words, and then relaxed as she realized his compliment was sincere. After he'd seated the women, he turned to Anna with a smile. "It's good to see you up and about. We've been worried about you."

Her face brightened as she raised her eyes to his. "If it weren't for your hospitality, I wouldn't be alive. I'll always be grateful."

G.W. flushed, embarrassed by her expression of gratitude. "It's little enough after what you've gone through."

They did not dwell on recent hardships, but talked instead about the weather and the price the wool would fetch in Sydney. Though Anna said little, Rebecca noticed how she studied G.W when he wasn't watching. It was likely that her contact with true gentlemen had been sparse.

After lunch, G.W returned to work and the women sat on the porch taking in the fresh air. Rebecca knew she'd guessed Anna's thoughts when Anna wistfully observed, "G.W. seems such a gentleman and so kind, too."

Rebecca nodded. "You won't find a nicer gentleman anywhere."

"I know," Anna said softly. "I've looked."

The next morning, Cole and his men hitched the bullocks to the carts for the long trip. Rebecca watched, fighting the forlorn feeling that swelled in her chest. Though he had not come to see her yesterday, she felt as though she was sending her heart with the dark-haired man.

He disappeared into the barn while the men covered the carts with oiled tarp. Rebecca swallowed hard and slipped through the barn door. Her eyes adjusted to the filtered light as she breathed in the scents of horses and grain.

Cole turned sharply, nearly bumping into Rebecca as he carried ropes to tie down the tarps. His eyes filled with uncertainty.

Rebecca hesitated. "I wanted to tell you goodbye. I'll pray for your safety until you return."

"You'll have G.W. to care for you." He wished he'd held his tongue when he saw her wince. He didn't want to hurt her. Yet his long day of thought yesterday had done nothing to improve his mood, and he couldn't stop the heat of jealousy that burned in his heart.

Rebecca's eyes filled with tears. "You have no reason to be bitter toward G.W He doesn't know how we feel."

"I hoped you would set him straight. Instead, I think you plan to keep us both as suitors."

She brushed a tear from her cheek. "That's because you sometimes frighten me. There's a part of you that's cold and unforgiving. I worry that it will come between us."

Cole's eyes narrowed, and his lips tightened into a thin grim line. "Come between us? Yes. I suppose it might. You tell me that forgiving Finley will keep me safe and give me peace. That's asking the impossible. He killed my mother and I won't forgive that."

Rebecca studied him. Suddenly, she was struck by inspiration. "I lost a parent, too. And I forgave you the part you played in my pain. Yet, when I ask you to forgive Finley, you can't."

Cole felt as though an invisible power had rocked him onto his heels. He stared at her dumbly as the truth of her words sank in. He had accepted her forgiveness and had even admired the sweetness of her spirit.

Had he been in her place, could he have been so forgiving? He knew with a sinking feeling that nurturing his hatred had helped make Finley the monster he had become. If Cole could not get rid of his anger, how long would it take before he became like Finley in other ways?

Cole shuddered violently, the thought so repulsive that it nearly made him ill. "You're right," he whispered. His throat felt dry. "I don't deserve forgiveness if I can't return it. Perhaps it would be best for both of us if I stayed in Sydney and found work after I settle your aunt's affairs."

He brushed past Rebecca without looking at her stricken face. He needed time to think and to determine what he had become. He had never felt more unworthy of her love or more incapable of doing what she asked of him in return.

Rebecca longed to follow him, to cling to him until the anguish left his voice and he promised to return. Yet what would that solve? Cole fought an inner battle that could be won only from within. She shivered, knowing the outcome would determine if they would spend their future together.

The crunch of footsteps on straw made her catch her breath. Ned stepped from a far stall where he'd been feeding the horses. His expression left no doubt that he'd overheard what had been said.

Rebecca's hand fluttered to her lips. "I didn't know you were here."

The old man's forehead puckered into a frown. "I'd have to have been blind these last weeks not to have noticed your feelings toward Cole. At first I didn't like it. Though I've changed my opinion a lot about him, he's a troubled man, my girl. I still wish G.W. was your choice."

Rebecca caught her lip between her teeth. "I know it seems hopeless. G.W. seems such an obvious choice. But I can't help how I feel. I've tried, Ned. I truly have."

The old Scotsman came forward, his lumbago adding a limp to his step. "Ye have no feelings for G.W.?"

"Only as a friend. I know you and my father hoped I would feel more."

Ned rubbed a hand across his bristly white beard. She looked away from his probing gaze, feeling like a schoolgirl caught cheating during a test.

When he spoke, his chastening made her wince. "I've been thinking ye've not been completely honest with G.W., letting him believe there's hope when there's none."

Rebecca shook her head. "That was never my intent. He's just the sort of man I should want for a husband. I've been hoping, in time, that my heart would agree."

"What will ye do if it does not?"

Rebecca looked away. "I don't know. I suppose I would rather marry G.W. than end up alone. I couldn't bear the loneliness if Cole doesn't return."

Ned took her hand in his gnarled fingers and gave it a gentle squeeze. "Yer thinking there's something ye could have said to change his mind?"

"I wish I could make him see the peace he could have if he let go of his hatred."

"Give it some time. And give the Almighty a chance to work."

Rebecca nodded at his wisdom. When the carts were ready to pull out, she hugged him and kissed his wizened cheek. As she drew away, he held her gently by her shoulders and gazed affectionately into her eyes. "Yer the daughter I never had, Rebecca. I want ye to be happy. I want to draw my last breath carving toys for yer children."

Rebecca's eyes were drawn to the cart that Cole urged forward. He gave her a brief nod before turning away. The pain and confusion in her heart tore at her, making her ill with the fear that he would not return.

She turned back to Ned and lowered her eyes, embarrassed by her inability to hold back the tears that welled behind her lashes. Struggling to keep her voice steady, she said, "If Cole chooses not to return, I will make every effort to place my affections with G.W. Perhaps, someday there will be children on this porch." She nodded toward G.W.'s house.

To her surprise, Ned patted her hand and said, "Don't give up on Cole yet. He'll not find peace in Sydney."

She wanted to believe him. Yet, as they rode away, a sense of foreboding gripped her. She shook away her anxiety and returned the wave Ned gave her before she turned for the house.

She met G.W. on the porch and they entered together. She was surprised to see Anna waiting for them in the sitting room. She had brushed her dark hair until the red highlights shone, then twisted the strands into a neat bun.

Anna smiled timidly at G.W. as she tried unsuccessfully to smooth her wrinkled skirt. "Pardon my appearance, Mr.

Sanders. I left the rest of my clothing behind in my hurry to escape." A pretty flush crept into her cheeks.

Rebecca sighed, knowing her own clothing was equally in need of laundering. Perhaps they could wash their dresses in the evening and let them dry overnight.

G.W. rubbed his hand across his chin. Then he said thoughtfully, "I don't know why I didn't realize that you both lost everything when you came here. Of course you need new clothes. You rest up today while I take Rebecca to Bathurst to pick out material for new dresses."

Anna shook her head. "I don't know when I could pay you back. You've done too much for me already."

Putting aside the disturbing fact that she already owed him money, Rebecca said, "I can pay you back from the sale of my wool." She wondered dismally if she would soon be enclosing marriage in the bargain.

G.W. smiled. "It will be compensation enough to see pretty ladies wearing new dresses."

He began eagerly to prepare for their trip, excited as a schoolboy about the promise of a day spent with Rebecca. Two of his men accompanied them for protection. The trip went smoothly, and when they arrived he left Rebecca to shop, saying, "We'll be at the livery stable. I'll come back in an hour to pay for your purchases. Will that be long enough?"

Rebecca feigned insult. "Plenty of time for a woman who knows how to make up her mind."

She smiled at him and then went about her task of choosing for both herself and Anna. She took her time, enjoying the leisure of picking out the best colors for each of them. She was only just finishing the addition of thread and other necessities when G.W. returned.

The trip back was long and hot. Rebecca endured it stoically, to show Anna the fabric.

They arrived back in late afternoon. Rebecca thanked G.W. for his kindness as she carried the wrapped bundles into the house. Anna ran her hand across the smooth pastel fabrics as though caressing a treasure.

"I supposed the men passed their time in the saloon while you shopped?" she asked.

Rebecca frowned, distracted by her plans to draw up a pattern for her new dresses.

"No. They chatted with Gus at the livery stable."

Anna wore a thoughtful expression on her face. Rebecca watched her as she drifted away to place the fabric in her room.

For the next few days, they spent all of their spare moments working on their new wardrobes. Anna proved a more masterful seamstress than Rebecca and finished her dresses several days sooner. Rebecca joined her on the porch one afternoon to admire her neat, even stitches as she mended one of G.W.'s shirts.

"I'm doing some sewing to help pay for my keep."

Rebecca smiled. "It's a good thing I'm feeding the animals instead of mending. My aunt tried for years to teach me to mend, but I never got very good." She studied her hands, large and clumsy compared to Anna's delicate fingers.

"I wish I had earned a living as a seamstress instead of working in a saloon. No decent man will want me now," Anna said.

Rebecca shook her head. "It's not true. We can start over at any time to lead a new life."

Anna's voice trembled as she slipped the needle into a frayed buttonhole. "I'd like to believe that was true."

"You can believe it. And you can be a seamstress if you like. And any number of good men will be glad to marry you."

Anna nodded. Her dark eyes held veiled hope. "I'll think on that."

"Good." Rebecca said, firmly.

At dinner, G.W. cast an approving look at their new

dresses. "You two look so pretty, you make me feel like I should eat with the sheep."

Rebecca laughed. "A handsome man like you?" Though she was pleased to see his ruddy face flush with pleasure, her heart ached with the painful reminder that she really wanted Cole to see her in a new dress.

At the end of dinner, G.W. told Anna, "Rebecca reads poetry on Saturday nights. I know she'd be pleased if you'd join us."

Rebecca caught her breath. "I forgot all about it."

Anna fingered the ruffle at her throat. "I don't think I'd fit in. I don't know much about poetry."

G.W. covered her hand with his own large palm. Anna tensed, sucking in her breath, as he said, "I never knew the beauty of words until Rebecca came along. I'm sorry now for wasting so much time not knowing what I was missing."

Anna blinked quickly and nodded. "All right. If you want me to come, I'll come."

Rebecca read for an hour and then retreated to the deserted kitchen, where the wooden bathtub had been placed for the women to take their Saturday bath. When she emerged, damp and relaxed, she found G.W. and Anna sitting together on the porch, deep in conversation. They hushed so suddenly at her appearance that she paused awkwardly, feeling suddenly enlightened by the flush on their faces.

"Join us, please," G.W. invited. "We were catching a little breath of evening air."

As G.W. began an easy conversation recounting his busy day, Rebecca cast covert glances at Anna. There was no doubt that Anna held G.W. in high esteem. And she was not unattractive. Did he find her equally so? She pondered this possibility, suddenly realizing that G.W. had asked her a question. She stared at him, trying to think what he had said, but it was no use.

His brows gathered into a worried frown. "Are you feeling all right? You look a little preoccupied."

"I'm fine." She knew her assurance lacked truth. She had been tense ever since Cole left. But as she met G.W.'s concerned eyes, she knew it was time to get over Cole and lend her assistance to what she hoped was a budding romance.

Pleading weariness, she decided to leave them to themselves. "I'm going to bed a little early. Goodnight."

As she lay in bed, listening to the crickets, Rebecca felt more alone than she had since her father died. One thing was certain. She did not want to spend her life with only the sound of crickets as her only nightly company. Yet if Ned came home without Cole, she would have to face that possibility. She closed her eyes against the pain in her heart as she drifted off to sleep.

When Rebecca came to breakfast the next morning, Anna was already at the table. Her dress of pale blue cotton gave her skin a satiny glow, her face showed little trace of the bruises and cuts that had disfigured her. She poured coffee for G.W., and Rebecca was glad to see she was regaining her strength.

Her good humor was a sharp contrast to the despondency that had engulfed her when she first arrived. She smiled easily as she chatted with G.W. Rebecca listened, thinking that he was just what Anna needed. He treated her like a lady, and she responded with the devotion that he deserved.

After breakfast, Rebecca fed the animals and tended to the orphaned lambs. She returned to the barn to find G.W. saddling two horses. She paused in the doorway.

A rosy blush crept up his neck as he said, "I thought fresh air would do Anna good. Would you like to come, too?"

Rebecca shook her head, relieved that the second horse was not for her. "No. I've got work to finish." In truth, she did feel like being alone.

They returned late in the morning, happy and flushed from the heat. Rebecca smiled as she listened to Anna's report of her ride. G.W. had been right about the outing. The fresh air had given sparkle to her eyes and a glow to her cheeks.

As they sat on the settee after lunch, mending clothes for the men, Anna said, "I've never known it could be like this. I feel like I have a family now."

Rebecca smiled. "I've always wanted a sister."

"I hope we always live close."

"Perhaps we will," Rebecca agreed. She poked her finger with the needle and sighed. As usual, her stitches started off well, but soon grew uneven.

Anna laughed as she took the rough shirt from Rebecca. "Let me finish this. Your stitches are much too long."

Cole sighed. It was only the first night of the long trip. Already, he felt grimy and tired from swallowing dust churned up by the carts' heavy wheels. While the other men sat at the fire to talk, he took out a small poetry book he had borrowed from G.W.'s library. With his back against a eucalyptus tree, he sat apart from the group and began to read.

He was not aware that Ned had joined him. When he sensed that he was not alone, he flushed with embarrassment and closed the book.

Ned watched him thoughtfully. After a moment of meeting the old man's discerning eyes, Cole said, "I miss her, Ned. And I'm tired of being angry. I want the peace Rebecca talks about, but I can't find it."

Ned nodded. "Ye've taken the first step by admitting your need. Now all ye have to do is convince yer heart to follow."

Chapter twelve

After Ned left, Cole lay restless in his bedroll. Finally he crept from his bedding. He felt too unsettled to sleep, and maybe a walk would help him relax. He strode away from the sleeping men, trying to escape the conviction that had lodged deep in his soul.

A hundred feet from camp, a large eucalyptus spread its welcoming branches. Cole headed toward the tree, taking time to study the glittering stars peeking from the velvet sky.

He gazed at the Southern Cross, feeling his chest tighten with emotion at the magnitude of the universe. The anger he'd held clenched in his heart seemed small compared to the vastness above him. He ignored the swarming mosquitoes that hummed in his ears. He knew that if he did not release his bitterness now, he would never do so. The decision was his.

Cole stared into the sky and realized he had no desire to carry his burden any longer. He wanted peace, not only to gain Rebecca, but for himself. For the first time, he realized how the hatred had eaten at him, casting its poisonous web around him until he had almost traded away the chance for happiness. But it would imprison him no longer. He would put his past behind him where it belonged. He determined to cast away his obsession for revenge and be haunted no longer by his personal demon. Taking a deep gulp of the night air, he exhaled the anger and bitterness he'd embraced for so many years. When at last he turned back to camp, he knew he would never be the same.

He slipped into his bedroll and buried his face away from the pack of hungry mosquitoes, and then slept with a peace he had never known possible.

The next morning, Cole had broken his usual habit of being the first one up. It took a hand on his shoulder to rouse him from sleep.

Lester grinned as he stared down at Cole. "You're harder to wake than Ned. You must be getting old."

Cole squinted into Lester's wrinkled face. He pushed himself up and replied, "I'm younger than you."

"You must have been having some dream." Lester turned away, eager for the breakfast of charred eggs fried in a blackened pan.

Cole noticed Ned watching him closely. He waited to catch Ned alone, and then grasped the old Scotsman's arm as he hitched the horse to the wagon. Ned turned expectantly.

Cole spoke in a low voice. "You'll never believe what happened last night."

Ned fixed him with a discerning eye. "Yer face tells me ye've made peace with yer past and ye'll never be the same." A slow smile spread under his grizzled whiskers.

Cole kept his voice low as he glanced at the men and nodded. "The biggest problem I've had is the way I've hated Finley, wanted to kill him. Last night my hatred melted into pity. He's building his empire on sheep and the blood of whoever gets in his way. He's losing his own soul."

Ned nodded. "Like a lot of people, power means more

to him than anything else. It's what he respects. He can't see why anybody would think different and he'll consider ye weak for giving up the grudge."

A curse from one of the men brought Cole's attention back to the job. He helped harness a balky bullock, then mounted his horse to ride in front of the four wagons carrying G.W.'s massive load of wool.

He thought of Rebecca and how pale her face had become when he spoke of staying in Sydney. Didn't she know that, even in his torment, he could never stay away from her? He couldn't wait to return and tell her he had released the anger that had blackened his soul. Like a thirsty man who had stumbled upon a pool of water, he wanted to spend his life enjoying the blessings of a home and family. Yet there were long days ahead before he could return and tell Rebecca the news.

Cole exhausted the stamina of both men and bullocks with his eagerness to reach Sydney and finish his business. Still, the days dragged by slowly. Talk turned to snug bars where tired men could trade tales about quagmires and spring downpours that trapped travelers and their wool for more than a week. The stories always grew more formidable with each telling as they were recounted over mugs of ale.

On the final day of the trip, it seemed more than Cole could bear to see the sky turn from pale blue to dusty gray. Clouds scuttled together in clusters, capturing the sun.

Thick-packed eucalyptus trees bent their tops together and rustled like a thousand whispering voices passing the secret of the upcoming rain. The men cast worried glances skyward, urging their lumbering teams forward before a cloudburst turned the rutted road to ankle-deep muck and delay their arrival.

In precaution, Cole halted the wagons in order to spread the heavy oiled cloths and lash them securely over the wool. He ignored a frilled lizard that scuttled across the path, heading for higher ground. The smell of smoke rose from chimneys in the city. Sydney was close, fewer than ten miles to the east.

As they resumed the journey, heavy drops of rain battered the cloth. Though the cover was waterproof, the travelers were not. The rutted path changed from cinnamon to a dark cocoa brown as drops joined to form rivulets between the ruts. The men pulled their collars tighter around their necks in a fruitless effort to keep out the rain.

"Take the wagons to the side of the road and tie the horses under the trees," Cole shouted, fearing a horse would lose its footing and go down.

The trees provided a break to the men and animals that waiting in the cover of thick leaves. The smell of eucalyptus permeated the forest, while koalas stared down with round black eyes, looking not at all bothered by the rain.

A trail of water spiraled down Cole's spine. He adjusted his hat and pulled up his collar, then hunkered down to wait while the downpour turned the humid forest air into the consistency of thick soup.

The deluge finally ended, leaving a curtain of fog rising from the steamy ground. Cole inspected the wagons. Each wheel had sunk into the muck.

He grunted in disgust. It would exhaust even the sturdy bullocks to drag the carts through mud that sucked at the wheels and pulled them back down into the soupy ground with each turn.

"We're not far," one of the young guards said hopefully.

Cole shook his head. "But we're too far to get there in time to sell the wool today. If I have to keep watch over the wagons, I'd rather do it here than in Sydney. We'll camp here tonight and finish the trip in the morning."

Despite the obvious wisdom of the decision, he was as disappointed as any of the men to postpone their arrival another day. It meant putting off the relief of getting the wool safely to market and receiving payment. But by pushing ahead they would arrive exhausted in the middle of the night. Better to wait and let the water recede. It would be rough enough going in the morning.

As the fingers of darkness reached into the forest, they found enough dry wood to start a fire and heat another night's worth of canned beans.

Ned grinned at Cole from the firelight. "I sure miss Rebecca's biscuits. She's a fine cook."

"I had my mouth set for a meal in town tonight," said one of the drivers.

"You'll get your meal tomorrow," Cole said absently. His thoughts were on what he should buy for Rebecca when he reached Sydney. She had lost everything in the fire. She could use cookware or material for dresses and linens. But she could find those things in Bathurst. He wanted to get her something truly personal.

With a quickening of his pulse, he knew exactly what it would be. He had been frugal with his pay, never gambling it away or spending it on idle pleasures. He could afford a proper gold wedding band instead of a silver trinket that would tarnish with age.

He swallowed hard as he tried to picture her reaction. When she learned he was a changed man, would she accept the ring with the joy he hoped to see in her eyes? She had admitted she loved him. All that had stood between them was his stubborn heart. But now . . .

The memory of his parting words filled him with a remorse that made his mouth go dry. What if she believed that he did not mean to return? Perhaps she would agree to marry G.W.

He stared moodily into the sooty darkness as though the urgency of his heart could hasten daylight and speed him on his journey. But no matter how quickly he wished to conclude this trip, they would spend a good part of tomorrow getting to Sydney and two days attending to business before they could begin the long journey home.

He lay in his bedroll and thought of Rebecca: her face, her hair, and her gentle smile. He imagined slipping the ring onto her finger.

"Wait for me, Rebecca. Please, wait," he coaxed silently in his mind as he drifted to sleep.

At last, the new day arrived. The remaining ten miles of the trip were difficult, just as Cole had feared. The bullocks strained to pull the wagons across the ruts. Both drivers and beasts arrived at the outskirts of Sydney mud-splashed and sweat-covered.

The wool buyers knew the quality of G.W.'s wool and haggled only briefly over the price before they reached a fair deal. After Ned and Cole received payment they supervised the unloading of the wool. It was accomplished quickly since the men were eager to clean up and get to supper and the games of chance that ran all night at the saloons.

Cole denied each request for advances on their pay. "Maybe I can't keep you from being fools, but I don't intend to share the blame. This money, all of it, goes back and you can collect your pay when it's due, as usual."

With good-natured grunts, the drivers saw their wagons safely to the livery and parted company with Ned and Cole.

Ned appraised Cole. "Ye look like ye had a fight with a mud bank and lost." The old man's lively eyes were filled with mirth.

Cole grinned back. "You don't look too good yourself."

"Aye. Maybe we should consider cleaning up before dinner," Ned suggested.

Cole nodded, trying to ignore the grumbling of his stomach as he glanced at his watch. "It's too late to see the solicitor this afternoon. I'll have to visit him in the morning. I wish we could start back after that. But I promised the men a full day of rest before we leave."

Cole chafed against spending an extra day in the city. But he knew the men would not be as good-natured about having their trip cut short as they were about an advance on their pay.

After a visit to the bathhouse, Cole sat with Ned in a quiet corner of the hotel restaurant. He realized how comfortable he'd become in Ned's company. And since neither of them cared for saloons, spending the evening together seemed only natural.

Ned raised an eyebrow. "If ye don't mind, I'd like to go with ye to the solicitor tomorrow. Rebecca's been worried that her aunt left a debt to be settled."

Cole shook his head. "I don't see how Rebecca could be held responsible."

Ned rubbed his grizzled chin. "I hope not. Fancy law talk can muddle yer head until ye can't think straight. I remember when Roger came back from trying to see his wife and Rebecca. Rebecca's aunt threatened to have her solicitor find a way to bring charges if he didn't stay away."

"Those must have been bad days."

"The worst." Ned's solemn expression brightened as he said, "The good days were when Rebecca was a wee girl growing up on the ranch."

He chuckled. "She caused a lot of trouble with all the critters she tried to tame. And I've never seen a lass ask so many questions. She shot them so fast, I felt like bullets were rattling in my head. But her smile could brighten the most rainy day."

Ned continued with stories of Rebecca's childhood. Cole grinned, thinking how Rebecca would blush if she were present. He was so engrossed with Ned's memories, he hardly noticed as the hour grew late.

When he finally sank into a dry bed, he succumbed immediately to the exhaustion of days on the trail. Suddenly, someone rapped softly on the door. Cole opened his eyes to the inky blackness of pre-dawn. He threw back the covers and slipped from the bed. The plank floor creaked its protest as he moved to the door and crouched, listening.

The hall was quiet. Only Ned's snores from the adjoining room broke the silence of the night.

Cole convinced himself he'd been dreaming.

Then he heard another knock.

He reached for his gun and held it ready as he slipped open the latch and peered into the dark hall. A gruff voice said, "If you're the fellow who was with that old man, I got something you need to hear."

Cole edged open the door, keeping his gun trained on the visitor.

"Who sent you?" he asked.

The man grunted. "I came on my own."

Cole cocked an eyebrow. He had come fully awake and was beginning to think clearly. "Is this about Ned?"

"It concerns both of you, if you'd like to stay alive. Can I come in?"

Cole stepped aside. He kept his gun on the stranger as he said, "Light the lamp so I can see you."

The visitor moved to the bedside table and lit the oil lamp. As his face flickered into illumination, Cole studied him. His thinning hair held a sprinkling of gray, as did his dark bushy beard. A slender nose rose from his thin face. Above the nose, two steel gray eyes appraised Cole in return.

"My name's Mattock," the man said. "I was playing cards tonight with a bloke named Jess. Seems he doesn't like you or the old man."

Cole's stomach soured at the news that Jess and his crew were still in Sydney. He'd hoped to avoid contact. But perhaps if their paths had to cross it was better here than on the trail.

"Did he give you a message?" Cole asked.

Mattock scowled. "I don't carry messages, especially for the likes of him. I'd swear he cheated me at cards, but I can't prove it. His kind are lower than a snake."

Cole nodded. "That describes Jess."

He regarded his visitor with a growing respect. The man carried himself with a proud air of independence. His linen shirt and breeches were neat, if not expensive. He didn't seem the sort to be bought by Jess.

The stranger shifted on his feet and Cole noticed the tired lines under his eyes. He nodded to the chair and said, "Have a seat and tell me what happened."

Mattock lowered himself stiffly into the chair. Cole sat facing him on the end of the bed. The older man ran a hand across his beard before saying, "After the card game, I overheard Jess talking to the bloke with him. Seems they watched you ride into town, even found out what room you were in. Someone named Finley wants you both dead. When Jess got drunk, he spilled the plan."

Cole's eyes narrowed with anger. "And how does he propose to kill us?"

"He plans to wait for you and the old man to come out in the morning, and then accuse you of a gambling debt. He says you always wear your gun. If he draws, you'll reach to defend yourself."

Cole head swam with confusion. "Jess knows I'd beat him in a draw."

The man nodded. "That's why he hired a professional gunman to sit in the window of the room above you. As soon as you draw, this bloke's going to take you down. Then Jess can shoot the old man and claim he caught a stray bullet."

Cole drew a shallow breath. The ignoble plan reeked of Finley's greed. With Ned out of the way, it would be harder for Rebecca to rebuild her ranch. Finley hoped to force her to sell.

Mattock stood to take his leave. "I hope you believe me. I don't like their kind. I'd like nothing better than to spoil their plans."

Cole shook his hand. "I'll be careful. Thanks for warning

me." He took a bill from the top dresser drawer and offered it to Mattock. "For your trouble."

Mattock shook his head. "I don't need money. I'm good at cards and I'm honest. Just keep Jess from getting what he wants."

Cole nodded. "Nothing would please me more."

In a grim mood, Cole went back to bed and dozed lightly until daylight. Without waking Ned, he roused his men, who were bunking together down the hall.

"Get up. And don't tell me you're too drunk."

Cole's tone brooked no argument. The men rubbed their eyes and squinted into the faint sunlight that stained the wall a pale pink. Cole's muscles tensed with impatience as he waited for them to wake up and listen to why he'd waked them after only a few hours of sleep.

With their bleary stares focused on his face, he explained, "Jess hired a gunman to kill me and Ned. I'm thinking we'll change his plans."

They sobered quickly as Cole told them about Mattock's visit. When they'd gathered guns and ammunition, Cole led his men up the stairs. "We'll disable the gunman first, and then take care of Jess."

Only the faint squeak of boots ascending wooden stairs testified to their presence. They reached the third floor and Cole crept to the door. He heard someone moving around in the room.

He knocked softly, and the movements ceased. In the quiet he could hear a gun being cocked.

A low voice demanded, "Who's there?"

Cole muffled his answer against the door. "It's Jess."

The door opened a crack and the men piled against it, knocking the occupant backward. He fell with a heavy thud, his arms flung above him. Before he could regain his aim, he was pinned by the men and relieved of his weapon.

The gunman's eyes narrowed to angry green slits. Wasting no effort in struggling, he scanned faces for the man in charge. His gaze rested on Cole.

"You better have a good reason for this." His voice held death.

"I do," Cole replied. "I want to stay alive."

He turned to the men. "Keep him here until I meet Jess in the street. Then make sure he checks out of the hotel and heads out of town."

Lester followed him to the door. "Maybe one of us should come with you."

Cole shook his head. "I can handle Jess on my own."

He stopped to collect Ned and found the old man dressed and waiting. He grinned when he saw Cole. "It's about time ye got up for breakfast."

"I've been up awhile and so has Jess."

Ned's smile faded as Cole crossed the room and peered down at the street. His puzzlement grew as Cole said, "Sit down and I'll tell you what I've learned."

Ned shook his head when Cole finished. "I should have known Finley would never let things be. He won't rest 'til there's blood spilt."

Cole brushed his finger across the scar near his eye. "Then he'll be disappointed, won't he?"

They stepped from the dim interior of the lobby into the early sun. Jess lounged against a post across the street, seemingly relaxed. Cole saw him stiffen when they emerged.

While Ned lingered near the hotel, Cole strode into the street. It was quiet at this early hour. Soon businesses would open and wagons would clog the road.

Jess glanced at the third-floor window, and then walked forward, positioning himself.

"I have a debt to settle with you," he called to Cole.

"Before you draw there's something you should know. Your hired gun is upstairs with my men. There's no one to help you."

Jess's long face drained of color. He glanced at the window, beads of sweat breaking on his brow. His hand wavered above his gun.

"Don't be a fool, Jess. No matter how much Finley wants this done, it isn't worth dying for."

"I don't intend to die."

Cole saw naked fear in Jess's pale eyes. Yet with stubborn indecision, he held his ground.

"You know I can beat you," Cole stated. Cole's reputation of accuracy and speed with a gun was well deserved.

Jess's hand twitched and Cole drew swiftly. He felt a primitive rush of adrenaline as his gun cleared the holster. For a split second, he considered putting the bullet in the center of Jess's chest. A week ago he would have made that shot and taken pleasure in doing it.

But he'd changed. He no longer had to settle every debt. His heart had been freed of the bitterness he had carried.

He fired into the dirt in front of Jess's feet. Jess froze. His mouth slacked open as his knees swayed. The certainty of death showed in his eyes.

He stared at Cole, waiting. His fingers twitched reflexively. Cole's eyes narrowed.

"Take your hand off the gun. I could shoot you right now and walk away free. But I'm not going to shoot you. I'm going to let you go back and tell Finley it will take more men than he can hire to get rid of any of us. Now walk away."

Jess kept his eyes riveted on Cole as he backed away, as though expecting to feel the impact of a bullet at any moment. When he disappeared around the corner, Cole turned to Ned.

"I hope I don't regret letting him stay alive."

"Life and death are not our choices to make. You did the right thing."

After making sure that his men had dispatched the gunman, minus his weapon, Cole had breakfast with Ned before walking the block to Bridge Street, where the solicitor was.

A young man opened the door, staring down his slender nose while they stated their names and nature of their business. He ushered them into an outer room decorated with lavish imported rugs. The thick maroon of the carpet carried swirled patterns of gold embossing.

A carved settee sat against one wall. Opposite the settee was a small teak desk with a ledger opened to keep account of the day's business. The young man offered them a seat and then disappeared into an inner office. The murmur of voices drifted to the sitting room.

The young man reappeared, fluttering nervous fingers across the papers on his desk. He adjusted his thick glasses and peered at them.

"Mr. Peters will be with you shortly. May I bring you coffee?"

Ned and Cole declined.

A mantle clock ticked loudly above the fireplace. Outside, the town had became alive with the sounds of shouted conversations and passing wagons.

Cole shifted restlessly. He was too used to activity to feel relaxed in a cramped, stuffy room. Only the reminder that he was doing this for Rebecca kept him on the settee. His heart swelled with love, knowing he would return to her as soon as he settled her business.

The young man busied himself at the desk. At last, a distinguished gentleman with a silver mustache appeared in the doorway. His gray suit was professionally cut to fit his bulky frame.

He greeted them with a booming voice as he shook hands and invited them into an office dwarfed by a massive polished desk. When they were seated in two high-backed chairs of gold and blue tapestry, Cole set Rebecca's letter on top of the polished desk. "Rebecca Dalton has sent her permission for me to settle her aunt's affairs."

The solicitor's dark eyes appraised him as he reached for the letter. He read it carefully, then cleared his throat. "As you must know, Miss Dalton spent several years living in her aunt's house before returning to her present location. During that time, her aunt had the wisdom to see that she was usefully employed."

He paused to lace his beefy fingers together. "Miss Abigail had the generosity to set aside the girl's wages against a time when she might need them."

Cole blinked at the unexpected words. He glanced at Ned, whose face showed equal surprise.

Mr. Peters ignored their exchanged looks and continued. "Miss Abigail lived frugally so that Rebecca might have a savings to fall back upon. This money, along with the sale of her aunt's house, has added up to a handsome sum. Since you have been appointed to carry this money to Miss Dalton, I shall assume you are prepared to guard its safe arrival."

Ned turned to Cole. "Aye, 'tis Providence to get it now when the ranch house needs to be rebuilt."

Mr. Peters sniffed haughtily. "It's the providence of Miss Abigail, I would say. But I shan't quibble with you. Are you prepared to accompany me to the bank to sign the money into your hands?"

Cole nodded. He rose as Mr. Peters pushed himself up from his desk.

"How much money will Rebecca be receiving?" Cole asked.

Mr. Peters eyed him as though the question was in poor taste. "Miss Abigail managed to set aside a little over forty pounds in case her niece should show the ill judgment of her father and come into difficult circumstances. She quite disapproved of Rebecca's return to uncivilized country."

Cole held back a smile, trying to hide his delight in Rebecca's good fortune from the stern solicitor. Instead, he replied, "Miss Dalton will be grateful to her aunt for her sacrifice."

"As she should be." Mr. Peters nodded his large head; his thick lips remained pressed in disapproval.

They returned to the outer office to find the apprentice still bent at his papers. He glanced up expectantly as Mr. Peters said, "I will return as soon as I escort these gentlemen to the bank."

The young man nodded and returned to his work.

Cole was glad to depart the stuffy office where the air had felt heavy in his lungs. He took a deep breath of the mixed scents of animals, bakeries, and tanning shops that lined the busy street. It felt good to be moving again, restoring circulation to his legs and pumping fresh air into his chest.

Mr. Peters concluded their business with efficiency, shook hands again, and departed for his office. Cole tucked the thick bundle of notes into his pocket and kept his hand near his gun. Even though the business had been conducted in the privacy of an office, he worried that word of the extra cash he carried would get out.

While Ned went for a haircut and trim of his beard, Cole hurried to the jewelry shop. He had told no one about his plans. He wanted Rebecca to be the first one to see the wedding band he picked for her.

He took his time looking over the rings until he settled on the perfect width of shiny gold. He paid with his savings and placed the ring in the pocket with Rebecca's money.

The responsibility of being the sole guard for both Rebecca's and G.W.'s money weighed heavily on Cole as he returned to the hotel. Every footstep, too close behind him, made him edgy. He drew his gun as he ascended the stairs, not wanting a surprise when he reached the second-floor landing.

To his relief, the halls were quiet. Most of the guests had headed to an early lunch or business about the town.

He knocked on Ned's door. Ned didn't answer.

Cole slipped into his own room and latched the door. He sat on the bedside chair and withdrew the ring, holding it in the light to delight in its luster. How beautiful it would look on Rebecca's finger.

He grinned, knowing he would be unable to keep the surprise from Ned. Impatient now, he waited for the old man to return.

The sun rose high in the sky, then headed for the western horizon. Cole listened for the sound of Ned's footsteps in the hall.

Another hour passed.

Puzzled by the delay, Cole knew he had no choice but to see what had become of the old man. He trudged toward the barbershop. As he passed an alley beside the boarding house, he saw a crowd gathered. Nudging his way to the front, he saw an old man lying on the ground, his white hair and beard painfully familiar to Cole.

Chapter thirteen

Rebecca sat near the open window. The oppressive heat that hung over the ranch during the day made her appreciate the early morning breeze that ruffled through her thin cotton gown. Too soon, the breeze would surrender to the scorching tyranny of the sun.

Voices drifted from the bunkhouse as the men stirred to life. She let the familiar sounds wash over her as she scanned the road leading from the ranch. Ned should return soon, bringing money from the sale of their wool. Thoughts of his return should have brought relief. The money would allow them to rebuild and move back to the ranch. Yet the prospect of moving back brought her more anxiety than joy.

She shifted restlessly, examining the choices that were left to her if Cole did not return. If he remained in Sydney, lost to her forever, then she was a fool for not having wed G.W. when she had the chance. He was a good man. She and Ned were safe here. If she returned to her ranch, Finley could come back to burn them out or kill them.

But she did not regret her decision, especially now that she had seen the way Anna and G.W. looked at each other. Even if G.W. felt honor-bound to respect his proposal to her, she could never let a selfish desire for security stand between two people who were so clearly attracted to one another. She cared too much for both of them. And she was convinced that, feeling as she did for Cole, she could never make G.W. as happy as the woman who looked at him as though he had descended from Mount Olympus.

For the first time, she seriously considered selling out to G.W. and returning to Sydney. Ned could stay on here. Then she would not be responsible for any harm that might come to him if they chose to live at Finley's mercy.

Rays of sun streamed into the window. She blinked at the brightness, not having realized how late it had become while she sat lost in thought. She brushed her sleep-mussed hair in long determined strokes, wincing as the brush encountered a tangle. Then she slipped into one of her new dresses and hurried to breakfast.

She found Anna and G.W. already at the table, sipping coffee and talking in hushed voices. Rebecca paused, feeling again like an intruder. Anna spotted her and gave Rebecca a bright smile. "You look pretty and refreshed."

"Thank you. I could say the same for you."

G.W. grinned as Rebecca settled into a chair beside him. "I'm a lucky man, with two beautiful women to look at each morning. I could get used to this, you know."

The women exchanged pleased looks. Rebecca said, "After thinking about all the trouble of rebuilding, I realize I've become quite spoiled. Life here has been much easier than having to chase sheep around my own ranch."

She caught her lip between her teeth, wishing she had bitten her tongue. Would Anna and G.W. take her careless comment to mean she was hinting at a proposal?

She looked down at the breakfast plate Davies brought and wondered if the silence that followed was as awkward for the others as it was for her. When she glanced up, G.W. had finished his breakfast.

"I'd best get out to the pasture to check that young sheep

who was ailing yesterday. What will the two of you do today?"

"We invited the men to pile any clothes that need mending onto the bunkhouse steps," Anna answered.

"Ah . . ." G.W. quipped. "So I've got unclad men out tending sheep today."

The women chuckled at the image, melting the tension.

"I hope it hasn't come to that. Perhaps they'll manage to find one outfit without a tear," Rebecca replied.

"For my sake, I hope so." G.W. dusted his hat and joined the men as they finished breakfast in the kitchen.

Anna turned to Rebecca. "Shall we collect the clothes? We can carry them back in the laundry tub."

Rebecca sighed. "I'd much rather be out tending the sheep than stuck in the house."

Anna grinned. "G.W. wouldn't think of asking a woman to do men's work. I find that refreshing."

Rebecca made a playful face. "You would. You enjoy sewing."

When they'd collected the clothing, they sat on the porch to catch the meager breeze that failed to cool the air. Rebecca glanced at Anna, pleased to see the healthy pink glow in her cheeks. Her bruises had healed, and her face showed no trace of either the physical or emotional abuse she'd suffered. Tranquility, often touched with humor, filled her dark eyes.

Rebecca cast about for a way to bring up the subject of G.W. If Anna truly loved him, she would never have to leave the protection of the ranch. For that, Rebecca would be grateful, for there was little opportunity for a young woman to begin a business in Bathurst, the closest town.

Yet she knew she would have to tread carefully. She knew from experience that Anna was proud and rather private about her thoughts. She studied Anna's graceful fingers as she pulled her needle through a ragged buttonhole. "You've been happy with your new life, haven't you?"

Anna smiled. "Happier than I've ever been."

She decided to judge Anna's reaction by saying, "I've been thinking. There's not much honest work for a woman in Bathurst, but I could put you in touch with the women whose wash I did in Sydney. Surely they need mending, and once you got enough work, you could open a little dress shop."

Anna bit her lip. A tell-tale rush of color stained her cheeks. Rebecca rushed ahead. "There's no hurry, of course. G.W. seems happy to have you here."

Anna blushed. "G.W. is a gentleman. He has treated me with more kindness than I could ever repay."

Rebecca leaned toward her. "Then it is just as I thought. You do care for him. And I believe that he cares for you." She sighed, adding, "And that makes you a very lucky woman."

She hesitated, and then felt she could no longer contain the anguish in her own heart. She longed for female advice about her feelings for Cole. "I fear I am not so lucky. I know what it's like to love and not be sure that you are fully loved in return. I fear that Andrew Finley will always come between us."

Anna's hands froze above her work. Rebecca could feel her friend's eyes scrutinizing her face. "That was my fault."

Rebecca looked into Anna's eyes and was touched by the depth of her concern. She felt a pang of remorse at having mentioned her destroyed home. She placed her hand reassuringly on Anna's arm. "No. It wasn't your fault. Please don't feel bad."

Anna's pale face made Rebecca wish she wouldn't blame herself for Andrew's evil actions or Cole's violent reactions.

After a moment, Anna asked quietly, "Would you marry him if he asked you?"

Rebecca sighed. "He has asked, and, Anna, I don't know. I don't know what to do. It has all gotten so complicated."

Anna brushed loose threads from her lap and said, "Yes, I can see that now."

Rebecca waited for her to make further inquiries, to offer to give advice. Instead, Anna sat solemnly rigid in her chair. Rebecca studied her, puzzled.

Anna suddenly rose from her seat. She avoided meeting Rebecca's eyes as she said, "Perhaps I should go and see if Davies needs help in the kitchen."

Rebecca was disappointed. She had longed to confide the whole story, and she had made Anna uncomfortable. She chastised herself for bringing up Andrew. Anna's wounds were still fresh, and it had been callous of her not to think of it.

She glanced at the stack of mending that lay at her feet and wished she had never begun talking. Anna was considerably quicker at the task and Rebecca had hoped they would complete the job together.

To Rebecca's consternation, Anna continued to avoid her all day, pleading a headache and taking lunch in her room. G.W.'s concern was evident when Anna was still absent for supper.

"Do you think she's sick?" G.W.'s face puckered into a frown.

Rebecca sighed. "I don't think so. I made a reference to Andrew that I think upset her. I didn't mean to."

G.W. nodded, his gaze sympathetic. "Maybe a ride tomorrow morning in the fresh air would make her feel better."

Rebecca nodded. "Maybe so. I'll check on her before I go to bed."

She knocked on Anna's door after supper and entered at her invitation. Davies had left a supper tray from which Anna had eaten very little.

Anna sat near the window, staring into the darkness. She turned briefly, forcing a smile for Rebecca before turning back toward the night. Her dark eyes held a strange resignation.

"I'm sorry, Anna. I never meant to upset you. Please forgive me. I won't mention Andrew again."

"Andrew?" Anna turned to her, puzzlement on her face.

"Yes. It upset you when I brought him up."

"Oh . . . yes," Anna nodded. "Is that what you thought was wrong?"

"Yes. Was I mistaken?"

Anna hesitated. She smoothed the fold on her lavender dress. "I do feel bad about the fire."

"But there's something else, isn't there? I said something else that bothered you. What was it?"

Anna looked away. "It doesn't matter."

"But it does." Rebecca felt her voice waver with emotion. "During the time we've been together, talking and sewing, I've felt like you could be my sister. I don't want to do anything to hurt you."

Anna's eyes filled with tears. "That's exactly how I feel. That's why I can't tell you. I would never want to come between you and happiness."

"Anna, dear, I don't see how you could do that."

"And until you do, I won't reveal what's in my heart. So please go now and don't ask any more questions. Make my apologies to G.W."

"He was hoping you'd like to go for a ride in the morning," Rebecca said softly.

Anna's small jaw quivered, then clenched in determination. "No. Tell him I don't feel like riding."

Rebecca laid a gentle hand on Anna's shoulder and sighed as Anna turned her face to the breeze that ruffled her curly dark hair.

"I'll tell him. But, tomorrow, please tell me what's wrong."

Rebecca found G.W. at his desk in the parlor, carefully examining a business ledger. He looked up as she approached. The pale glow of the lamp lit his face. Instead of his usual cheerful expression, his brows were drawn in concern.

"Anna?" he questioned.

"She still won't tell me what's bothering her. She doesn't want to ride, either."

She waited for G.W. to suggest a course of action. Instead, he studied her with a solemn expression. "Perhaps I know what's bothering her. I'll talk with her in the morning."

Rebecca nodded, feeling too tired to question him. Maybe tomorrow he would succeed in convincing Anna to share her feelings.

She lay in bed and closed her eyes. The creak of boots and the soft closing of the front door told her G.W. had closed his ledger and headed to the bunkhouse. Worry about the change in Anna gnawed at her, keeping her awake. Deep in her heart, Rebecca felt an ache of rejection. She had thought they were so close. They'd spent hours together. Rebecca had come to believe there was very little about each other they could not share. Rebecca wondered if her own preoccupation with her feelings for Cole had made her insensitive to clues that would explain Anna's strange behavior.

Her determination to think it through grew, and she puzzled on it as the minutes slipped by. She fell asleep with these questions still in her mind and awoke to the sound of parrots engaged in a noisy conversation outside her window. She opened her eyes to see Sunday sunlight spilled across the furniture, giving the dark wood of the dresser an amber glow. She sighed deeply as she stretched and remembered last night's conversation with Anna.

Rebecca pulled herself from the bed and began to dress. A knock at the door made her jump. She opened it a crack to see Anna standing outside. Her dark eyes were ringed with shadows. For a moment, Rebecca felt tongue-tied.

Anna usually went straight to breakfast, arriving before Rebecca. Her appearance could only mean she wanted to talk.

Rebecca recovered her senses and invited her into the room.

To her surprise, Anna blurted, "It seems we are in love with the same man. And, Rebecca, I do not want to come between you and the man you love. Until you make up your mind about marriage, I'm going away, to Bathurst, or maybe Sydney."

For a horrified moment, Rebecca stared at Anna in shock. "What about G.W.?"

Anna blinked back tears, and then composed her face into the mask she had worn when they had first met on the stage. "I feel terrible about this after all you and G.W. have done for me. He's never been anything but a perfect gentleman to me, one of the few I've ever known."

"Then why . . . ?"

"Please, Rebecca, can we just go to breakfast together?"

Rebecca followed, too stunned to refuse. Since she had never spoken of Cole, Anna must have read her feelings in her face. But she had been so sure that Anna loved G.W. And yet, any woman's attraction to Cole was understandable. Hadn't his handsome face captured her own heart?

She did not believe that Cole returned Anna's feelings. Instead, her heart ached with the thought of what Anna would be giving up if she did not stay here with G.W. Anna had certainly blossomed since she had arrived at the ranch. She was comely enough to attract suitors in Bathurst or Sydney. But would everyone expect her to go back to what she had done before? Rebecca shuddered. Surely now that Anna had experienced respect and kindness from a man she would settle for nothing less. Yet how could Rebecca criticize her for falling in love with Cole instead of G.W. when she had done the same thing herself?

She hoped at this very moment that Cole was camped somewhere, making his trip back to her. Thinking of the miles that stretched between them made her lonely. Even the early birdsong that usually comforted her brought her no cheer this morning.

G.W. was already at the table when they arrived. A quick look at his face told Rebecca he'd spent a restless night. They ate in silence after an awkward attempt by G.W. to inquire whether they had slept well. He lingered while Davies cleared the plates.

"I've looked forward to a ride this morning. Will you change your mind?" G.W. asked Anna.

Anna shook her head. "I have a headache. Perhaps Rebecca would like to go."

Rebecca frowned. She could tell that G.W. wanted to speak to Anna. Why had Anna suddenly become so cool?

She turned to Anna and said, "I don't feel like riding. You go ahead. It would do you good."

Anna pressed her lips into a stubborn line. "Do you really think that is a wise idea?"

Rebecca stared at her. "Of course."

Anna shrugged. "If it would make everyone happy, I'll slip into my riding clothes."

G.W. rose briskly. "I'll saddle the horses. A ride is exactly what Anna needs."

While they were gone, Rebecca sat at the dining room table and tried to compose a record of the assets that had been lost in the fire. Her pain over Anna's confession consumed her, interrupting her concentration until she finally sighed and set aside her efforts.

She rubbed her forehead as Davies clattered the breakfast dishes. She decided she could use some fresh air when his bellowed chorus of a sailing song proved more than her nerves could bear.

Rebecca perched on the porch railing and stared in distraction at the white dots of sheep on the horizon as she considered how confusing her life had become. Most of her confusion led her to a dark-eyed man who held her heart in impossible bondage.

She rose hopefully when Anna and G.W. returned. When they dismounted, Anna's slumped shoulders and tear-stained cheeks rent her heart. A look at G.W.'s face told her that words had passed between them. Had they disagreed?

She reached out to Anna. Anna turned aside, covering her face as she rushed into the house. Rebecca started to follow, only to feel G.W.'s restraining hand close gently on her arm.

Surprised, Rebecca tried to shrug him off. "I've got to see what's wrong."

G.W. shook his head. "We've got to talk."

The determination in his manner checked Rebecca as she stared into his troubled eyes.

He returned her gaze with steady sincerity and said, "I'm a simple man. I don't know any way to put this except to say it outright. Anna believes that you are in love with me. And she would never do anything to hurt you. And though I'll honor my proposal to you, I'd like to ask Anna to marry me if you're not going to accept my offer."

Rebecca felt her breath catch in her throat. She swallowed hard as bits of her conversation with Anna passed through her mind. How could she have been so thick-witted?

"It is *you* she cares for," she whispered.

G.W. nodded. He ran a hand through his sandy hair. "I have feelings for her, too. I knew I needed to know your plans when she told me this morning that she was planning to pack up and leave."

Rebecca gasped. "Leave? She has no place to go."

G.W. nodded. "I told her you hadn't given me an answer. She feels bad after all you've done for her to be the one to come between us."

"Please forgive me. This has been a terrible misunderstanding." Remorse filled Rebecca's heart. G.W. had deserved an answer long ago and she had put him off. Holding him in reserve like an island of security had hurt two people she held very dear.

"I'm sorry, so sorry," she whispered. "I should have declined much sooner. I hope you and I will always be good friends, but we are not in love."

He took her hand and pressed it gently in his own. "Will you tell Anna? She won't believe it unless she hears it from you."

"I'll tell her. And she will believe me. You and Anna deserve the happiness you've found. And I could not be happier for you."

G.W. released her hand. "Thank you. You'll always have a special place in my heart."

The relief on his face inspired Rebecca to action. She rose and walked to Anna's door. At her knock, she heard stifled sobs cease. As she entered, Anna wiped her eyes and sat up quickly. She shook her head. "There's nothing you can say. I've made up my mind to go."

Rebecca perched beside her on the bed. "But there is something to say. And I want you to listen. I don't love G.W. I never have."

Anna sniffed. "I don't believe you. You're being noble and trying to step aside. But I could never live with myself if I let you. You don't even have a house because of me."

"Ned and I will rebuild the house. Your place is here with G.W. He loves you and you love him." She drew a deep breath and continued, "You misunderstood me when we spoke on the porch. I was not talking about G.W. There is another man who holds my heart."

Tears unwillingly filled Rebecca's eyes. "He may not ever return. Our situation may be hopeless, but I can't help loving him."

Anna stared, uncomprehending for a moment, then

clasped Rebecca's arm. She sucked in her breath as she studied Rebecca. "Then it is Cole?"

"Yes, though I believe he is no more attainable than the wild horse I once loved."

"Oh, Rebecca, I am so sorry for not understanding. When I thought it was G.W., I felt my heart would break. But you were trying to tell me about your own heartache."

Rebecca bit her lip as Anna continued, "I could never be happy if you were not. I'll go to Sydney and bring him back if I must."

Rebecca smiled, brushing away a tear that slid down her cheek. "I believe you would, Anna. You truly are as dear as a sister. Now, wash those silly tears away while I tell G.W. to meet you in the sitting room for a proper proposal."

Anna smiled. "Thank you," she said simply.

Rebecca nodded and left the room. She found G.W. waiting anxiously on the porch. She smiled at his expectant face.

"Anna is waiting for a proper proposal."

Like a flower budding, his concern evaporated into the bloom of a smile. "Come in and have cider with us to celebrate."

Rebecca shook her head. "You two should spend this time alone. Anyway, I'd like to go for a ride."

G.W. frowned. "Not by yourself."

Rebecca tossed her head. "I won't go far. And I'll watch out for Andrew's men."

G.W. hesitated, glancing at the deserted bunkhouse. "I don't have anyone to send with you since half the men are gone to Sydney and the other half are working the sheep."

"I won't take any foolish chances."

He nodded, still looking unsure. He handed her his long-barreled pistol. "At least take this. I assume you can still use it. Roger used to brag that no young girl shot better."

Rebecca's eyes misted at the memory of her father's lessons in marksmanship. She could still feel his hand on her shoulder and hear his words of advice. To his delight, she had proved a quick learner with a steady aim.

Her mother had disapproved until the afternoon a tiger snake decided to sun on their porch. In her father's absence, Rebecca had dispatched the snake. With pride, Roger skinned the dead snake and tanned the hide to make Rebecca a belt. After that, her mother never said another word about guns being a danger to her daughter.

Rebecca anchored the weapon in her belt and turned away from G.W. She strode purposefully toward the corral, hoping a peaceful ride would help get her confused emotions under control.

She chose a gentle mare, saddled her, and set off at a lope across the rolling plain of grass and saltbush. The horse's hooves pounded a steady rhythm that echoed the refrain in her mind. *Alone . . . alone . . . alone . . .*

G.W. and Anna would have a home and family. They would be happy together. She begrudged Anna nothing. It was time the girl had a chance for happiness. And Rebecca was not in love with G.W.

Yet it hurt to know he was no longer eagerly seeking her hand. She had been unfair to keep him waiting and now she had run out of time. Even if she wished to marry him, he was in love with Anna now.

If Cole did not return, she would eventually be all alone. *Completely alone.* She tasted the salty tears that ran down her cheeks.

Even if Cole returned, they might never be together. Thoughts of standing by watching him grow more bitter as the years passed tore at her heart. Perhaps it was better if he did not come back at all.

She drew a sharp breath as a flash of dark clothing caught her attention. Despite her best intentions and her promise to G.W. she had ridden farther afield than she had intended.

Rebecca drew her horse to a halt. Her heart thudded in her chest. Had she been seen? She sat still as a bird, trying to see if the man was alone. He moved into full view under a far patch of spreading eucalyptus. Recognition came swiftly. Pale eyes, dirty blond hair. It was Finley's foreman, Jess. If he saw her he would surely attempt to drag her to Finley's ranch.

She breathed rapidly, weighing the risk of trying to hide with that of turning her horse and dashing back to the ranch. Could he catch her? Though she was armed with G.W.'s pistol, she had no desire to use it. She shivered, feeling a trickle of sweat snake its way along her spine. Before she could make a decision, she saw a second horse emerge from behind the tree. A brown-skinned man sat on its back. His hands were tied awkwardly behind him.

Her heart skipped a beat as she saw the noose that encircled his neck. With no time to compose a plan, she rushed forward in the hope of saving Wally.

Chapter fourteen

At the sight of Rebecca, Jess's eyes narrowed from surprise to cruel anticipation. He waited, unmoving, as he watched her approach, raking her with his gaze, violating her senses until her skin crawled with revulsion. Rebecca's stomach knotted. She touched the pistol that lay hidden in the folds of her skirt as she pulled to a stop a dozen yards from the men.

"Well, if it isn't Miss Dalton. A pleasure to see you all alone."

Rebecca bristled at his assumption that she would be helpless. She nodded toward Wally. "Get him off that horse."

Jess's eyes narrowed at her tone. Heartless eyes. They reminded Rebecca of Finley.

He shook his head. "I have a right to hang him. He stole a lamb off the boss's place." He pointed to the pitiful creature lying in the grass.

Rebecca sat tall in the saddle and faced Jess. "You're on G.W.'s land now."

Finding his voice, Wally said, "It was dead when I found it."

Jess turned his fierce gaze on Wally. "I chased this thief

across the boundary of our ranch. He stole and he's going to pay. And as soon as I'm through with him, you'll pay too for interfering."

He reached for the noose and Rebecca jerked the pistol into sight. Though her heart pounded so hard it shook her ribs, she held the gun steady, pointed at the center of Jess's chest.

"Wally said it was already dead. I'm a good shot and I don't miss. Now help him down," she commanded. Her voice surprised her by its steely tenor, though her mouth felt dry.

For a moment, Jess studied her. She met his eyes with unflinching determination. Then, seeming to accept that she was serious, he jerked Wally roughly from the horse and watched as the weakened man stumbled toward Rebecca.

Jess studied her with the cold eyes of a creature she would only expect to meet deep in a murky ocean. Then he said, "You think you've won. But you've lost. You'll find out how much you've lost when G.W.'s men get back."

Anxiety tightened Rebecca's chest. "What do you mean?"

Without a backward glance, Jess turned his horse, leaving her question unanswered.

Rebecca slipped from her saddle and untied Wally's hands. "Climb on behind me," she said.

Not being a frequent rider, he looked uncertain.

Rebecca shifted impatiently. "You can't stay out here. He might circle and come back."

Wally mounted reluctantly and held tightly to her waist as they cantered back to the ranch. Rebecca arrived out of breath to find G.W. loping toward them, his sandy brow puckered. "We were getting worried," he said anxiously.

"I had to stop Jess from hanging Wally."

G.W.'s stunned expression slowly gave way to an angry flood of color.

Wally slid from the saddle as G.W. said, "If he comes onto my ranch to pick off one of my men I'll order him shot on sight."

Rebecca shook her head. "You can't do that. He was on Finley's ranch when Jess found him."

G.W. turned a stern gaze on Wally. "What were you doing on Finley's ranch?"

"Hunting goanna. The lamb was dead when I found it. No reason to let it go to waste."

Rebecca sighed at the aborigine's insistence that no one could own the land. "You have to stay off Finley's property. If you don't, there's going to be trouble. You'd be dead now if I hadn't ridden up when I did."

Wally nodded. His lips parted in a grin. "I'm glad you came."

Rebecca couldn't help smiling. "Me too. But promise you'll stay off Finley's ranch."

Wally nodded. Rebecca doubted he could manage to keep the promise. She handed G.W. his pistol. "I'm glad you made me take this along."

He holstered the gun and said, "Anna will be glad to see you. She's been put out with me for letting you go riding alone."

Rebecca nodded. "I'll go right to her."

She watched him ride off to supervise his men, hoping that he and Anna would be spared any pain at Finley's hand. Yet she knew in her heart that she and all of her friends were on a collision course with the greedy rancher.

As she walked her horse to the corral, Rebecca saw Anna waiting on the porch. She scurried to meet Rebecca.

"Are you all right?" she cried.

Rebecca nodded. She tried to steady knees that felt suddenly weak. "I had a run-in with Jess." A cold lump of fear at his parting words had lodged in her heart.

"Andrew's foreman?"

"Yes. He was going to hang Wally for retrieving a dead lamb from Andrew's land."

"He's not as bold as Andrew, but he's more devious in his own way," Anna said.

"He said that he had done something terrible that I'd find out when the men got back. What do you think he's done?"

Anna shook her head. "It's just a threat. Don't worry."

Despite Anna's reassurance, Rebecca found it impossible not to worry. She concentrated her energy on a thorough sweeping of the living room while Anna began to dust. As they worked, Rebecca tried to concentrate on Anna's happy prattle.

"I never thought I could be so happy. Imagine me, about to be a respectable married woman." Her dark eyes shone.

Rebecca smiled. "I can imagine it very well."

"I've always wanted children, but I wanted to raise them better than I was raised. G.W. will make a good father, don't you think?" Anna flushed becomingly.

Rebecca swallowed hard and answered, "He'll make a wonderful father."

She swept more vigorously, fighting the bitter tide that rose inside her. At this moment, she wished she were Anna, even in spite of her past. Though they held the same dream, only Anna's would come true. Anna would have a devoted husband to replace her loneliness. Children would fill their house with laughter.

Rebecca imagined the small shack she would rebuild to share with Ned. It would not be the home she longed to create with a loving husband and children. Perhaps, like her father, she could not make life turn out the way she wished.

Anna stepped onto the porch to shake out the dust rag. A moment later, she flew into the room, her eyes bright with excitement. "They're back! And Cole is with them!"

Rebecca felt a vast wave of relief even as she chastised herself for her unbridled joy. They had solved nothing since his departure and her joy would likely turn to misery soon enough. But, for the moment, all she could do was drink in the sight of Cole, slumped wearily in the saddle. Her heart beat quickly with a mixture of hope and doubt.

She found herself shaking as Anna squeezed her shoulder and whispered, "I told you he'd come back."

As the group unhitched the empty wagons, Rebecca's eyes moved from G.W. and Cole to G.W.'s man seated on her own wagon. She glanced around the group, studying each face.

Her eyes locked with Cole's and she shivered, recognizing the same anguish she'd seen when he first met her at the coach. A feeling of dread gripped her as she forced her legs to carry her down the porch steps. The men fell silent, busying themselves with their work, yet she sensed their tension as they unloaded supplies and cared for the horses.

G.W. stood beside Cole. She studied their faces.

"Where's Ned?"

Cole drew a deep breath, his chest expanding with the effort. "I'm sorry, Rebecca. I found him in an alley. He'd been robbed."

She took a step back, swaying with the shock. "What are you saying?"

Cole licked his dry lips. "He's dead. He died of a knife wound right after I found him. His last words were concern for you. He asked me to take care of you."

The emotions of the last weeks welled into a painful maelstrom. She'd lost her father and she'd lost Ned. Since Ned had been robbed, she'd even lost the money to rebuild. It was too much to bear. And somehow it all seemed to be Cole's fault. Surrendering all attempt at self-control, she sobbed, "First my father, now Ned. Do you bring death to everyone I love?"

She ignored the anguish in Cole's eyes. She had loved him and he had brought her only pain. Rebecca wished she'd never met him, never known he existed. She turned

away from G.W.'s open-mouthed shock and rushed past
Anna into the house. Slamming her bedroom door behind
her, she flung herself onto the bed. Sobs tore painfully at
her throat. She had come here to find relief from her loneliness. Now she was alone and penniless, a burden to the
man who had first taken her in.

G.W. would soon have a new wife. She had no place
here. Rebecca sat up and dried her eyes on her skirt, trying
to think clearly. She was tired of loss and tired of dashed
hopes. With no money and no will to keep up the fight,
she knew she had to sell her property to G.W. She would
return to Sydney and hope the money would last while she
sought work. Perhaps she could clean and wash for the
people who had employed her when she lived with her
aunt. The thought that Finley would not get her ranch gave
her some satisfaction.

A knock at the door interrupted her thoughts. Rebecca
caught her lip between her teeth. She knew she had shocked
everyone by her savage outburst, and now she felt ashamed.

More rapping at the door, slightly louder, let her know
her visitor had not gone away.

Rebecca wiped a hand across her damp cheeks. It was
likely Anna. Anna would want to comfort her. Though her
intentions would be good, nothing could right her collapsed
world.

Before she could reply, Cole twisted the knob and
stepped through the doorway. His face was tense, but the
determination in his eyes captured her attention.

She stared at him and wondered at her odd sense of de-
tachment. Since she had come here, she had borne pain and
suffered loss. Now that there seemed nothing left to lose,
her emotions had gone mercifully numb.

Cole knelt beside her and said, "You can hate me if you
like, but I want you to know I had nothing to do with Ned's
death. Finley hired a man to kill Ned. The first try failed,

but I wouldn't be surprised to find out that he was behind the robbery."

Rebecca stared past Cole and said, "Jess told me I'd find out what I'd lost. I never thought he meant Ned. He was like a second father to me. I never expected Finley to kill him to keep me from rebuilding." Her voice sounded wooden to her ears.

She sought Cole's eyes and read his anguish. He released a shuddered breath and said, "Ned and I became very close on the trail. He was the only one who knew when I finally released the bitterness that I've carried so long. You can't imagine my relief at being rid of that burden. It's like being released from a dark prison cell into the warm rays of sunshine."

Rebecca placed her hand tentatively on his arm. "I'm glad for you. If only you had done it sooner . . ." Her voice choked with a sob. With poverty to face and so much pain behind them, was it too late?

Cole pulled her gently to his chest and held her. She cherished the comfort of his arms, the feel of his fingers as he stroked her hair. She could feel the strong beat of his heart. The scent of trail dust rose from the shirt that grew damp from her tears. Rebecca wanted to stay with him forever, to make this memory last a lifetime.

"We have a future now, Rebecca," Cole said steadily. "I have a long way to go, but I can honestly tell you, if you agree to marry me, you'll be getting a new man. I'll help you rebuild. We'll make the place something your father and Ned would be proud of."

Rebecca drew back and wiped her eyes. "I don't have money to rebuild. You said Ned was robbed of the profit from the wool."

Cole smiled. "Apparently you misjudged your aunt. She left you all the savings you earned and whatever else she tucked away. It's more than you could need."

Rebecca gasped. "Aunt Abigail saved my money? She never said a word."

"It seems she feared your determination to run your own life would lead you to hard times some day and you would need the money. Apparently she was right, though not for the reason she expected."

Rebecca drew a ragged breath and attempted to calm her uneven breathing. "I guess she loved me in her own way."

Cole ran a finger gently along her cheek. "She's not the only one who loves you. Say you'll marry me."

"I can't." Her words were barely a whisper. "I want to but I can't."

Her answer sent his mind reeling as though from a hard punch. He studied her face, composed now, yet devastatingly sad. Cole had known Ned's death would be a shock. Yet he assumed that once he confessed his changed heart, she would accept his proposal. Wasn't that what she had wanted?

He swallowed his fear and said, "You said my bitterness was keeping us apart. That's not true anymore. Don't you believe me?"

Rebecca's eyes brimmed with tears. "I do believe you," she said softly. She clasped his hands tightly in her own. Her eyes attested to her sincerity.

"Then what is it?"

Rebecca pulled away from him and faced the window. "I've lost enough men, Cole. If we stayed here and tried to rebuild, I'd lose you too. Finley killed Ned. If you stand in his way, he'll kill you also."

Cole opened his mouth to protest, only to close it quickly. She was right. If the two of them tried to rebuild and raise sheep, it wouldn't be long until Finley had him murdered. He shuddered to think what would become of Rebecca, alone at Finley's mercy.

The emotion drained from her voice, making her sound remote, as she said, "I'm selling my property to G.W. and going back to Sydney. I've had enough of death and broken dreams. I'd rather live alone than face more loss."

Cole put his hands on her shoulders and felt her muscles tense. "I'll go with you. I'll live in Sydney with you."

Rebecca shook her head. "Your life is out here. This is what you know. You'd be as miserable in Sydney as my father would have been."

Cole's grip tightened as he turned her to face him. "No more miserable than you. You love the sheep station. If we have to leave, we'll leave together. I can work as a wheelwright."

Determination shone in Rebecca's eyes. "No. I'm afraid of what you might become. I saw what life in the city does to men, the gambling and the drinking. I won't risk the pain of having you become a different man than the one I love here. It's better to remember what we had than to live in unhappiness."

Bitterness assailed Cole. "Through no credit to either of us, I've become what you wanted. Yet you say it's too late. You'd throw away what chance we have of happiness."

Rebecca's chin quivered as tears spilled down her cheeks. "I'm thinking of you, too."

Her stubbornness seared his heart like a hot poker. He would give up anything to be with her. And now that he could make a true commitment, she felt it her duty to decide what was best for him.

Facing her squarely, he said, "If you take no chances, Rebecca, you'll become a hard old woman like your aunt."

The shock in her eyes was his only consolation as he turned for the door. He would give her time to think. Perhaps tomorrow, she would see that he was right. If not, he had to bring her to her senses, make her see that she was wrong. His heart ached with the need to persuade her that they belonged together. If living in Sydney were the price for having her, he would go without a backward glance.

They would travel to Bathurst to see the visiting preacher and marry before traveling on to Sydney.

The next day the small party of mourners gathered at the spot Rebecca had chosen for Ned. The sun had just risen to push aside the curtain of darkness and burn away the gray mist that clung near the ground.

"He should have died peacefully of old age," G.W. told Cole in a fierce whisper.

As Cole watched Rebecca weep, he longed to wrap her in his arms and tell her he would always be there for her, that her future would be happier than her past.

Yet, Rebecca was careful to give him no chance. She avoided his eyes and spoke only to Anna. His hope that she would reconsider returning alone to Sydney sagged as he overheard her plans.

"I don't have much to pack, so I'll do it today. I can ride to Bathurst tomorrow and take a coach bound for Sydney the next morning."

"You'll stay at least until our wedding," Anna protested.

Rebecca shook her head, refusing to heed her friend's pleas. "It's better if I go soon. We all need to build new lives, you and G.W. here, me in Sydney. The sooner we begin the building the better it will be for all of us."

The group ate in awkward silence that evening. Rebecca remained withdrawn into herself, pale and stiff. When she excused herself right after supper, Cole fought the apprehension that gripped his heart like a vise. She was leaving, truly leaving, and she had reserved no place for him in her plans.

As the other men prepared for bed, Cole knew sleep was out of the question. He paced to the corral and stared into the darkness, seeking an answer. He wondered if Rebecca lay in her room equally restless and unhappy.

By the time he returned to the bunkhouse, he knew what he had to do.

Chapter fifteen

Cole rose for an early breakfast, and then hitched a team to the wagon. He listened to the staccato pecking of a yellow-tailed cockatoo as he waited impatiently for Rebecca to emerge from the house. The noisy bird gouged holes in a decaying eucalyptus to find grubs hidden beneath the bark. The darkness inside the eucalyptus reminded Cole of the darkness that had once filled his heart. He was a new man now, and he was determined to convince Rebecca that he could be everything that she wanted him to be.

He jerked alert as she appeared on the porch, clutching a small borrowed valise. Anna hugged her in a tearful goodbye while G.W. turned his hat in his hands. Deep furrows of unhappiness pleated their brows. G.W. glanced at Cole. "I see you've already hitched the team. Keep a sharp watch."

Cole's eyes fastened on Rebecca's pale face. "I'll take good care of her." His tone underscored his commitment.

Rebecca turned to G.W. "Thank you for all you've done. I'll sell you my land as soon as I have the papers drawn."

G.W. awkwardly clasped the hand she offered in his large palm. "Be sure to write and let us know you're all right."

She nodded. "You write, too. I want to hear about your wedding. This land will always be my home."

A sharp spear of pain pierced Cole's heart. Rebecca belonged here, with him. Would her stubborn heart lead her to the city, perhaps to marry a dandy there? The threat of lonely years stretching ahead threatened to overwhelm him, but he pushed the fear resolutely aside.

After a last tearful hug from Anna, Rebecca allowed Cole to assist her into the wagon. She turned to wave a final goodbye as Cole guided the wagon onto the rutted grass trail.

He glanced to the side to see her straighten her shoulders and press her lips into a tight line. But the quiver of her chin betrayed the fact that she was not as composed as she pretended.

"I'd like to visit my father's grave if you have the time before you leave me in Bathurst," she said softly.

Cole nodded. "I'll spend as much time with you today as you'll allow."

Rebecca turned away to drink in the pastoral scenes of kangaroos and emus resting under the shady branches of eucalyptus trees. Cole knew she was trying to imprint the images on her heart before facing the sentence she had imposed on herself. She felt that her only choice was to live with no family ties in a town that held only bad memories. Yet leaving her beloved outback was tantamount to leaving part of her heart. She was going back a defeated woman, and it hurt him to see her so.

They reached Rebecca's property and halted near Roger's grave. Cole helped her alight and stood at her elbow as her eyes roved from the grave to the sight of the burned-out house.

"It's gone. All the dreams I lived for in Sydney are gone."

Cole's heart beat fast as the words tumbled from his

mouth. "I truly believe we are meant to be together. I love you and I would go anywhere to be with you."

Rebecca's composure crumpled as tears rolled down her cheeks. "I dreaded seeing you today because I knew I couldn't trust myself to hold firm in my decision. But Cole, don't you see? You are like that beautiful horse I could never have. You don't belong in a city like Sydney any more than that stallion belonged in a corral. And it's too dangerous for us to stay together here. There really is no choice. Don't you see?"

Cole took her gently by the shoulders. "I went to Sydney with thoughts of staying. It was you who brought me back, not my dislike of the city. I release you with a full heart, as you did me. But if you go without me, I'll send a letter every day for the rest of my life asking you to let me join you."

Rebecca's eyes were azure pools of grief. Entranced by their depth, Cole did not notice the riders descending the low rise beyond the trees until the pounding of hooves drew his attention.

He heard Rebecca's sharp intake of breath and knew that her fear echoed the apprehension pounding within his own chest. He gave her a gentle shove downward and ordered her to stay on the ground. Dread gripped his heart as he recognized Finley, Jess, and several other riders, including Sam, who had once been his friend.

He ducked behind the back wagon wheel and aimed his gun. If he fired a shot into their midst, he might be able to panic their horses. To his dismay, G.W.'s horses bolted instead, taking the wagon that had protected them. The riders pulled to an abrupt halt to jeer at the hapless pair.

"Look who we have here," Finley crowed. "You got good eyes, Jess, to spot these two leaving G.W.'s ranch."

"And trespassing on what's fixing to be your property, Boss," Jess replied.

"This property will never belong to you," Rebecca replied through clenched teeth.

Finley's hard eyes appraised her. "You don't have a choice." He swiveled toward Cole. "Drop your gun or we'll kill her right now."

Cole tossed down his gun. He knew Finley was more than capable of carrying out his threat. Murder meant no more to Finley than killing a sheep. He felt his hopes sink as he surveyed their situation. He was unarmed and outnumbered by the men. Without a miracle, he and Rebecca were surely doomed.

With a creak, Jess swung down from his saddle and retrieved Cole's gun. Rebecca cried out in alarm as he pointed the weapon at Cole. Sweat dripped in Cole's eyes as he steeled himself for the impact of the bullet.

Before he could shoot, Finley intervened, "Not like that, Jess. I have a better plan. A little wagon accident is in order." He glanced at Roger's grave and raised an eyebrow. "And at such a fitting place." He turned to Sam. "Bring back that wagon and break the wheel to look like there was a crash. Then we'll put their bodies next to the overturned wagon."

Cole stared at Sam with sudden insight, realizing that it was not his own carelessness that had caused Roger's wheel to break. He felt sickened by the discovery. His eyes glittered with accusation as he faced his old friend. "My carelessness didn't cause Roger's accident. You broke the wheel, knowing I would be blamed."

Sam scowled. "I had nothing to do with the murder. He was dead when they brought me there to break the wheel."

Finley nodded to Sam. "He did such a good job with the wheel, no one ever guessed the truth."

Rebecca's shook with a mixture of fright and fury. "And what is the truth? You owe it to me if I am to die at your hands."

Finley stared down at her from his horse. "Jess and I

overtook your father on the way to his land." He nodded at his gun and continued. "A blow to the head knocked him unconscious before he had the unfortunate fate to hit his head on a rock. And now you're going to die the same way. With you gone, there's no one to inherit the land. It's free for me to move in."

He gestured to the men who rode with him. "Get over there and hold Cole. He's about to have an accident. And, in good time, so will Rebecca."

His implication drove all rational thought from Cole's mind. He could not leave Rebecca to die at Finley's hands. In desperation, he charged at Jess.

A shot missed him. Enraged, Finley shouted at Jess, "Don't shoot him, you fool! It has to look like an accident."

The men charged in. Cole ducked as one of them swung the butt of his pistol, landing a blow to his neck that knocked him to his knees. Cole forced himself to his feet. Arms grasped at him as he swung violently. He connected with a chin. The blow produced a curse. But it wasn't enough. Bodies pressed forward, pinning his arms to his sides.

Rebecca screamed his name as she struggled to escape Jess's grip and reach him. He could not let them subdue him. He could not desert her.

Cole wrenched violently as they pulled him to the ground, driven mad by the knowledge that all was lost if he failed to break free. In a few moments someone would succeed in rendering him unconscious.

The sound of a shot diverted the men's efforts. They gaped at Finley, waiting to see what he would say. As his surprise faded, his face contorted with rage as he stared hard at Sam, the timid wheelwright, who had dared to pull a gun on him.

Sam spoke softly, yet his words were clear. "I'd welcome an excuse to kill you and I don't mind dying for the privilege. Either way, I won't let you kill Cole." Resolve was etched on his round face.

Finley spat. "You don't have the guts. You're nothing but a drunken worm."

Sam nodded. "I'm a worm that can put you where you won't hurt helpless women and children."

Jess released Rebecca and raised his gun. With a desperate cry, Rebecca shoved him with all her might, triggering a shot that skimmed past Finley's horse. The massive animal reared, throwing his rider into the air like a monstrous rag doll. Finley landed with a sickening thud and lay still, his head at an odd angle to his body.

The men surged forward.

"His neck's broke," one announced in a hushed voice.

Jess dragged his horrified gaze from Finley's still form to the barrel of Sam's gun. His gaunt face turned the color of fresh milk as the pistol slid from his hand.

Rebecca retrieved the gun and moved swiftly to Cole. Her breath came in uneven gasps.

"Don't shoot me, Sam," Jess begged.

"You're not worth the bullet, but I'll let Cole decide. You see, I figure Cole is the rightful heir to Finley's property. That makes him my boss. He decides what's done with no-goods like you."

Cole looked into Sam's expectant eyes as the truth sunk in. As Finley's stepson, he was the only heir to the sizable sheep station, boss of the men who had tried to kill him only moments ago.

"Get out," he growled at Jess. He swung his arm, encompassing the group. "All of you, get out and never come near here again."

With stunned faces, the men mounted their horses and headed toward Bathurst.

Sam holstered his pistol. His face broke into a wide, gap-toothed grin. He nodded toward Finley. "He didn't figure on me, did he?"

Cole let his breath out in a long shudder and realized his shoulders ached with tension. "It's good to see you again, Sam. I'm glad you were on my side."

Sam nodded. "I met up with a little fellow named Wally. He likes to poach on the ranch. He got me sober and told me what was going on. You were like a son to me, Cole. I didn't do what I should've to protect you when you were a kid. I was too beaten and drunk. But I wanted to make up for my past. When I found out the trouble Finley caused your pretty lady, I was determined to help."

"You made up for the past, Sam. How about staying on as my foreman?"

Sam grinned. "Be glad to." He looked thoughtful. "I suppose you will want to go tell G.W. what's happened. I'll take care of burying Finley."

Cole agreed gratefully and led Rebecca back to the wagon. Before helping her up, he asked. "Now that Finley can't threaten us, would you consider staying here instead of going back to Sydney?"

Rebecca nodded. "I could rebuild and not have to worry about being burned out."

Cole studied her solemnly. "I was hoping you would consider merging our ranches and becoming my wife."

Tears misted Rebecca's eyes. She wiped them away and gave him a smile that reminded him of sunshine breaking through clouds.

Turning mischievous, she said, "I can't think of anything I would like more than to stay here and become your wife. And I shall torture you dreadfully with my advice on running a sheep ranch."

Cole wrapped a possessive arm around her waist. "Oh, what sweet torture that will be." He stared down at her thoughtfully. "Do you think Anna and G.W. would like to have a double wedding?"

"I think they would be delighted with the idea."

Rebecca was glad of Cole's strong arms as he lifted her

into the wagon. Her heart still pounded from the recent terror. She couldn't believe such a few short minutes had completely changed the course of her life.

Cole became serious. "You know, I had no intention of leaving you in Bathurst. I was going to see you settled in Sydney, then come back every month until you changed your mind and agreed to marry me."

Rebecca smiled at his devotion, though her heart fluttered with the knowledge that she had almost repeated her mother's mistake. And now, though she had lost much since her return, she had the dream of a home with Cole, a dream that fulfilled her childhood longing. And though she had never succeeded in taming the wild stallion, she had succeeded in securing the love of her life.